Exploratory Tales

A Novel

Laura Clementz

Laura Clementz
Bright Communications LLC
Cleveland, Ohio

Exploratory Tales: A Novel
ISBN
Hard Cover: 978-1-7340497-8-7
Soft Cover: 978-1-7340497-6-3
eBook: 978-1-7340497-7-0

MIKITA

Tree Side Village

Mikita stands in the middle of the fitting area at the tailor's shop. Yash, the tailor, prepared the outfit himself. A deep pink, finely stitched tunic with horizontal lines of white and gold threads that create an attractive pattern. She twists to the side and makes sure the matching white linen crop pants fit just right.

Yash and Anya, the shop manager, appear from the backroom. Yash walks over to Mikita so he can tug and pull at specific places on the outfit and double-check the fit. "The colors really look nice on you."

"Yes, it looks beautiful." Anya smiles.

"I guess so. Anyway, the outfit is fantastic. It makes me very happy," Mikita poses like a model and giggles. "I'm so glad you guys are here. Aside from the department store, this shop is the only place to get nice clothes."

"That's what we do," Yash leans to the side and finishes his inspection. "Would you like to wear your new outfit home?"

"Thanks, but I will change back to my other clothes."

"Excellent. Anya will accompany you to the dressing room and we'll package it right away."

Mikita nods and heads for the dressing room, where she picks one of the three privacy areas.

Anya follows and stands outside the heavy curtain partition. After waiting a few moments, she says, "I liked what you were saying at spiritual practice services last week."

"What was that?"

"How you explained that a way to approach being more present is to just spend ten minutes doing nothing."

"Oh, yah?" asks Mikita.

"Yah. It was like getting permission to slow down for a short time. No thoughts about what needs to be done. Simple. I really like that idea."

"I'm so glad you liked the message." Mikita lets outs a loud sigh. "I have no idea how to tell my father I may not take his place."

"He's expecting that you do. You should talk to him soon."

"I know. I just…"

"Well, you would be an outstanding leader. Did you hear? Ellen opened her gallery; it's just a couple of doors down. You could stop and pay her a visit."

"Already? I didn't know she opened it yet. I'll have to check it out." Mikita pops her head out of the dressing room and hands Anya the new outfit. "Here you go."

Anya accepts the tunic and pants. "Excellent. We'll get it ready."

Mikita finishes getting dressed and walks to the store counter. Yash is packing the outfit into one of the tailor shop's bags. The bags are made of tan, high-quality paper complemented by deep blue-ribbon handles. He walks around the counter and to hand her the package. "Here you are, Mikita. Just let us know if it needs any adjustments."

"I'm sure it will be perfect as always. Thank you." She gives Yash a smile.

Mikita walks out of the shop feeling light and happy. She tucks the bag that carries her new outfit closer to her side. Anticipation fills her while thinking about trying it on with her white and gold beaded sandals. Her mind wanders further into the future, wondering if she would dare to wear the bright colors to Spiritual Practices Services.

As she walks down Main Street, she sees Mr. Reedy. Before she has a chance to extend a greeting, he says, "Hello Mikita. So good to see you."

"Good to see you also," she replies as they pass by one another.

Then, a woman she recognizes passes and says, "Hello Mikita."

"Hello, good day." Mikita smiles and nods.

At Ellen's new gallery, she leans over and looks through the window. Small paintings are neatly displayed on the large window ledge. They are sitting on decorative easels and more artwork covers the nearby walls. Ellen sees Mikita looking in and encourages her to come inside by waving her hand.

Mikita gives her a wave back and enters the gallery. Once inside, she looks around and shakes her head. "Whoa, Ellen! This is fantastic. You didn't waste any time."

"It really has come along."

"Absolutely. I'm so happy for you!"

"Thank you. I'm glad you stopped-in because I've been wanting to thank you. If it wasn't for our one-to-one sessions, I don't know if this would have happened," says Ellen.

"Thanks, but you did the work. You came to the community services. You completed the practices that fit. You dug inside yourself. I was just there to guide things along from time to time."

Ellen gives Mikita a sideways glance while saying, "Well, don't sell yourself short."

Mikita notices that the artwork is very earthy and accented by bright colors. They also range from impressionistic to abstract, depending on the piece. Drawn to a particular painting, she walks over to get a closer look. It looks like a floating sunset. When she gets even closer, she sees the half-circle that would be the setting sun has a variety of brown textures on its surface. The half-circle is surrounded by brilliant yellow, pink, and orange colors. Above that, the colors fade into darker shades of blue. Then the top of the painting looks like a twinkling star-filled night sky from a fairy tale. She asks, "What is the name of this one?"

Ellen walks over to admire the painting alongside Mikita. "This one is called *Consciousness*." Absorbing Mikita's interest, she says, "I especially like this one too. It came to me early one morning so, without thinking about it too much, I got to work."

After looking at the painting a minute longer, Ellen turns to the rest of the shop. "What's here is mine, but the rest of the side and back wall are for other local artists to display their work."

"Wow. What kind of art?" asks Mikita.

"Well, any kind. Thomas and I even talked about installing shelves and hanging mobile sculptures or glass art from the ceiling. I started an application process. We'll see what happens."

"Again, I'm so happy for you! This is wonderful, really wonderful."

"It's worth the work."

The scraping sound of the door pauses their conversation. Thomas comes in through the threshold with his fine blonde hair reflecting in the sunlight and broad shoulders barely clearing the narrow frame. He looks at Mikita and a gigantic smile takes over his face. "Mikita!"

Mikita leans back when he comes closer and opens his arms to give her a hug. "Isn't the gallery great?"

Mikita regains her normal posture. "Yes, your wife has made it happen."

He looks around. "She sure has… I also put a fresh coat of paint on the walls, made the easels, and hung the artwork."

"It is great," says Mikita with an affirming nod. "Well, I should really go now."

"We're so glad you stopped by the gallery. See you this weekend," says Ellen.

Thomas puts his arm around his wife and stands tall. "Bye Mikita, take care."

While walking out of the shop, Mikita reflects on how she had never seen both of them so happy and expressive. Lost in thought, she almost bumps into Emma on the sidewalk. "Oops, so sorry," she says.

"That's quite all right, Mikita," Emma says as she continues on her way.

She takes a turn down Livingston Drive, one of the nearest residential streets. As it has been for as long as she remembers, the scene quickly changes from shops, sidewalks scattered with people, and traffic moving down the street to houses lined with trees, sidewalks with children playing here and there, and parked cars sitting curbside. It's cooler in the shade of the trees, and it's the first time she thought about the warm sunshine that surrounded her when she was walking in town.

She walks deeper into the residential street and sees her parent's house where she still lives facing her at the end of the cul-de-sac. With a broad gaze, she absorbs how the house sits steady and silent, blending in with the green grass and large trees encasing it on the ample plot of land. Then her eyes focus on the rugged dark brown siding to where it meets with the front door of the sprawling single-story house. The lightness she felt while walking out of the tailor shop is gone, and a weight slowly covers her shoulders until they droop. She looks down to watch her feet take every step until she reaches the walkway to the house.

The Choice

Mikita steps inside the house and hears her mother, Caresse, moving around the kitchen. The clinics of pots and silverware fill the space. The door makes a muffled thump as Mikita gently closes it tight.

Her mother calls out, "Mikita, is that you?"

"Yes, Mama, it's me."

"Oh good, your father is looking for you. He's waiting for you in the meditation room."

"But Mama, I just picked up my new outfit. I want to see what shoes and stuff go with it best."

In reaction to her daughter's response, Caresse steps out of the kitchen to look at Mikita. She wrings her hands on the fabric of her apron. "Can you do that later? I think he wants to talk to you about upcoming services."

"Alright, I know. Let me put my things away first," says Mikita.

Simultaneously, Mikita turns down the hallway toward her bedroom and her mother turns back to the kitchen. When she walks down the hallway, the usual spots on the wooden floor make tiny creaking sounds. She passes her brother's bedroom door followed by the bathroom door on the other side of her, and she enters her little sanctuary. She flops the bag on a small armchair and sits on the edge of her bed. The surrounding leaves on the trees filter the sunshine and, with each breeze, bright spots dance around the room.

She closes her eyes and searches for her confident center that often gets lost when she's at home. Her stomach has too much weight in it, her chest feels tight, and there is a slight lump in her throat. Stretching the spine of her thin body upward and sitting tall releases some of the pent-up emotion. She continues by moving her head toward each shoulder, then rolling it in a circle a few times. Her eyes open and each hand spontaneously slaps the corresponding side of her thighs, encouraging her to rise from the bed.

Mikita brushes her long black hair away from her face and heads toward the meditation room in the back of the house. In the customary manner, she walks into the rectangular room and pauses approximately four soft steps past the doorway. Like the hallway, the floor is wooden, while the room is mostly bare, with bright white walls that match the ceiling. While waiting for her father, she examines the few detailed brass figures displayed on a wooden shelf. They change from time to time, but today there is the antelope who dances across the land, the skilled fish from under the sea, the beaver who lives both in and out of the pond, and the bird who soars through the air. Between each figure is a short white vase made of smooth-flowing ceramic full of neatly arranged fresh flowers.

On the other end of the room are wooden bookshelves filled with books. When Mikita scans the shelves, she sinks into a vivid memory. It was a sunny day, much like today, and she was a young child. She was being rambunctious and ran away from her mother to the meditation room where her father, Kitchwan, was practicing. He was sitting cross-legged on the large deck outside of the house with his back to the doorway, so he faced the trees and the outside world.

Mikita's burst into the room made Kitchwan abruptly stand-up, which stopped her in her tracks. She remained still except that her eyes stretched wide open. To her surprise, Kitchwan gently walked over to where she was standing.

"Why, Mikita, what is this all about?" he asked.

She shrugged and looked at him.

"Are you curious about the meditation room?"

Still shrugging, she swayed back and forth. "I don't know."

Her father stood tall and kept his eyes on her. Not knowing what to do, Mikita looked around the room until she noticed the bookshelves. Her eyes scanned up and down the wall of neatly arranged books.

He followed her gaze and gestured toward the bookshelves. "Do you like the books?"

She nodded and smiled. "Uh-huh."

Her father kept engaging her. "Many people created these books over many years. There is one book written by each spiritual leader of the village to remain for the generations to come."

Transfixed, she kept looking at the books. Her father bent over to meet her eye-to-eye before speaking again. "See, once they find their message, they work on one book for the rest of their life."

Mikita's eyes widened again. "The rest of their life?"

"Yes."

Her brow furrowed, and she turned to her father. "Then why aren't the books bigger?"

He happily chuckled. "You are a bright young lady!" He walked over to the vases with fresh flowers and pulled one out. Turning back to her, he said, "They work on them a long time, not to make them bigger, but as a spiritual practice. It's a way for us to grow wiser and make the message easier to read."

"Oh." Mikita's young mind was attempting to process her father's words.

He returned to her side and leaned over to present her with the purple flower. "Here, this is for you. Maybe one day you'll be a spiritual leader who leaves the next book, but for today, go and play."

Warmness rose-up her cheeks as she accepted the flower and, as abruptly as she ran into the room, she ran out the door.

Back in the present moment, it's taking her father longer than usual to acknowledge her entry. As most sunny days, he is in meditation on the back deck. Recently, he had paused his practice for a few days because he saw "the void." It was rare that he would deliberately stop his routine, but he also commented that he needed to allow his body and energy to readjust after the experience while his mind processed the broader perspective it had been given. When he returned to his routine, he changed from wearing the traditional flowing linens of light cobalt blue to cream ones signifying a deep change.

She knew little about the void except what she encountered while reading the spiritual texts. It's thought to be one of the highest achievements that only occurred to mature practitioners, and not every practitioner achieved that level of connection. They describe it as a deep, dark state where all thought disappears, and the ego becomes completely fluid to reveal pure consciousness. It's a passage to a high understanding of how intense compassion binds all things, especially those that appear as opposite. Even creation gives way to destruction, and destruction provides the means for creation.

Perhaps the recent changes are the reason her father is taking so long to rise from his meditation. But he had requested her to come. Mikita crosses her arms and stares intently at his silhouette. Then she shifts her weight from side-to-side, so her shoes and the floor softly squeak.

Kitchwan slowly rises from the mat on the deck and, with a fluid motion, pivots to enter the room. In the sunlight, Mikita notices how his black hair has become heavily streaked with shiny gray and white strands. He smiles at her, so his weathered tan skin makes wrinkles that flow from the corners of his bright eyes and surround his thin lips. He continues to smile as he walks into the room.

"Ah, Mikita, here you are. I wanted to plan for the next season of services. I had some thoughts about what activities the community might enjoy."

Her father motions towards the nondescript wooden desk on the other side of the room. It's so worn from years of use that it blends in with the floor. He walks to sit at the chair behind the desk. Mikita follows him and after he gets settled, she sits on the chair on the opposite other side.

Kitchwan pulls a folder out from one of the drawers. Before opening the folder to reveal a small stack of papers, he puts on his wire-rimmed glasses. Then he rummages through the stack and picks two sheets, laying them aside.

"I thought this time we would make a list of activities, then organize them over the entire season. That way we could have a distinct rhythm to the practices."

"The entire season?" she asks.

"Yes, we can still be flexible as things arise. It would be a blueprint, a guide. It could help us to connect with others in the practice to have a rhythm, an order to the activities."

"I see," she replies.

Mikita can't avoid the deep stare her father sends in her direction as he says, "I'm getting older and almost ready to finish my book. We could also work on a way to transition the services, so you progress to being the leader."

She lowers her head to stare at the folder on the desk and nods her head. She knows what his words mean. The silence spreads like a gas until it fills the room, and his deep stare penetrates to her insides while he waits for her to say something more. He sits more upright in his chair and asks, "Are you ready to write?"

Mikita can't prolong this moment any longer. In order to speak, she clears her throat so the words can get past tightened muscles. "Well, um… It's just that… I was thinking…"

"*Mik-keet-ahh*, my daughter, just say what's on your mind."

"I don't think that I'm the next spiritual leader for our village," she quickly replies.

"Why do you think such a thing?"

With a shake of her head, she says, "I am no teacher! I have nothing new or revolutionary to share with anyone."

To meet her line of reasoning, Kitchwan says, "We have been through this, no? You always have been very bright and are, once again, most correct. There are no spiritual teachers, only spiritual leaders in a sense we lead by example. We do this by continuing our practices, share how we practice and do our best to articulate the insights that come, but we always allow others to find their own path. It may take an entire lifetime or more, yet eventually we all end-up on the same road."

Mikita couldn't help but look at the ceiling, then bring her head downward in coordination with a roll of her eyes. "I know, father, but I feel like a fake, a phony. When I lead the spiritual practices, I'm nothing but a smiling actress on a stage."

With this statement, Mikita sees her father draw an expressionless face and close his eyes. She immediately knows he's practicing a simple technique to balance rising emotions. She contemplates if it's because her stance is unexpected or if his recent experiences have impacted something much deeper within him that he has yet to rectify.

He opens his eyes and continues, "I know what you mean. Yet, you connect with the community so well and it benefits from your leadership."

Mikita knew this wouldn't be a simple conversation. "Yes, I know. I understand."

"And you do not want to write?"

She bursts out, "That's just it! I don't understand the spiritual texts." She puts her hand on her chest. "I don't feel them." Then looking downward, sending a vibration of defeat, she says in a low voice, "Even after all these years, they don't speak to me."

"Alright. Let's just say you left working to become the spiritual leader of the village. What else is it you would like to do?"

"I don't know."

Her father's eyebrows raise, and he leans back in his chair. "Ohhhh… what you need is to go on an exploratory."

"An exploratory?"

"Yes, a journey away from home to find out who you are better. To find what you want to spend your life doing. Maybe even, to find your unique talent."

"Really? But to travel to the west, I would require at least two guides to cross the Great Mountains," she rebuts.

"No, no. You mustn't travel west. You will head east towards the grasslands and beyond."

Mikita shakes her head and furrows her brow. "Travel east? I don't understand. Very few have traveled to the east. Aside from what little is written about it in stories, it's uncharted land."

Her father smiles. "As always, you already have the answer within you. Travel to lands not well known to discover what is not well known inside of you, to discover who you should become." He stands, leans over, and points at her heart. "The answers out there will give you the answers in there."

Her eyes wide open with disbelief, Mikita stares at her father. Without releasing her stare or changing her expression, her mind contemplates how she has always known him to be an honest person. He never steered her wrong and, just as important, he could have reacted to their conversation in a different way.

Kitchwan remains standing until he leaves Mikita with her thoughts. He walks over to the bookshelf and scans a few shelves. Then he gently slides a book out of its home, and he takes it back to the desk. Finally, he sets the book down as he settles himself back in the chair. "If you agree, we will have a session early tomorrow morning that will bless your journey."

Unsure of how to respond, Mikita calculates that if she agrees, she can take some time to herself and could back out of it tomorrow. She returns his look and sits tall. With a slight bend of her head to the side and a nod, she says, "Okay. I will be here for the session early tomorrow morning."

"Excellent. I will speak with your mother and ask her to prepare the backpack with the necessary items."

⁂

When dinner with her parents and brother draws to a close, Mikita looks at her father and mother. "If you don't mind, I'm going to get ready for bed and retreat to my room for the evening."

"Of course, just rinse your plate," says Caresse, as she gives her daughter a motherly glance.

Mikita stands, places her silverware and napkin onto her plate to clear her setting from the table.

"Would you take the milk and put it in the fridge?" asks Caresse.

"Sure, Mama."

Reyansh, her brother, excuses himself from the table as well. "Can I go out for a game of catch? Douglas said he was going to get everyone together."

"Sure, clear your plate too," replies Caresse.

Reyansh almost plows into Mikita as she walks back to the dining room. She continues down the hall and stops in the bathroom to brush her teeth and wash her face. As she opens the bathroom door, she overhears her parent's conversation in the kitchen. Her hand pauses before flicking off the bathroom light switch when she hears her name. Then she stands silent, straining to understand what they are saying over the sounds of clinking dishes and water running in the kitchen.

"There have been some adjustments. Mikita is going on an exploratory tomorrow. I also instructed her to rely on you for the backpack," says Kitchwan.

The water stops running and her mother's voice clearly carries down the hall. "An exploratory, really? Do you think she is ready?"

"Yes, I think so. She agreed to go, but I sense she might not see it through."

"What brought about this idea?"

"She says that she doesn't think she is the next spiritual leader for the village."

"Yes, that would be a shame. She really gets on well with everyone in the community. They ask me about her all the time." The clinking of dishes and the sound of water running start again.

Mikita can still make out her father's muffled voice as he says, "I told her as much."

The noise of cleaning-up after dinner stops again and her mother says, "You know, I have noticed she has had other interests. She came home with another outfit from Yash's today. We have made it very comfortable for her here and have a very nice house with pleasant surroundings."

Mikita imagines her mother looking at her father with her knowing, one-eyebrow-raised expression.

He replies, "Um, yes. Perhaps the experience of an exploratory is an even better idea than I previously thought."

Mikita hears the familiar sound of the refrigerator door closing before her mother says, "I will make the necessary preparations and have a hearty breakfast ready just before sunrise."

With the conversation at an end, Mikita turns off the bathroom light and tiptoes down the creaky hallway to her bedroom.

The bright spots of sunlight on the bedroom floor fade until the remote illumination from streetlights take their place. After getting settled into bed, Mikita finds it impossible to sleep. Her mind races with all kinds of rambling thoughts. "*I've never heard of going on an exploratory. On top of that, traveling through the uncharted east? That sounds dangerous. Maybe I'm not ready.*"

She flops over and tucks the pillows in close. "*And anyway, what is the big deal if I like nice outfits? Sure, we live in a delightful house, but I've always kept my obligations with my studies and growing in the spiritual community. I haven't just loafed around or anything.*"

Still, she knew her parents loved and cared for her and her brother, so going through with the exploratory couldn't be that bad. By holding on to nice memories that flow in and out of her mind, she finally sinks into a deep sleep.

In her sleep, Mikita has dreams unlike any of the others she had before. They seem to be a jumble of scenes that appear in a variety of dull tones and bright colors with no corresponding noise or sounds. She's in a large blue space, as vast as the sky but deeper blue than the sky normally appears. The feeling of complete freedom encourages her to stretch out her arms and lean back. A breeze flows through her hair. The breeze escalates to a wind, and freedom turns into confinement and frustration. The frustration grows in intensity as streaks of bright lights, similar to streaks of bold lighting but thicker and more diffuse, develop all around her.

Then there are a series of about four or five black and white clips. She doesn't participate in the action, but watches as she encounters several eccentric people from different lands. They all wear outfits that seem like costumes. Some of them wear extravagant hats and accessories. While conveying what appears to be important messages, they exuberate happiness and light laughter. Each of them chatters on with a big smile while using exaggerated hand gestures.

Finally, she stands outside the house in the yard behind the back deck on a beautiful sunny day holding a flower. When she looks at the flower, her chest fills with an intense love. She recognizes it as the flower given to her by her father when she was a child, but the purple petals are barely visible. They only show themselves in the tiny spaces between the tight green leaves of the bud. The flower has not yet opened.

Mikita awakens to the familiar sights, smells, and sounds of her bedroom. The many scenes and emotions from the dreams run through her mind. After stretching her body, she has a sense of invigoration that urges her to jump out of bed and start the day. The details from the previous day reemerge. She remembers that she must meet her father for a session that will bless her exploratory. It's time to get ready.

She walks to her closet and wonders what one wears for a long hike. She looks longingly at the bag with her new outfit packaged inside but picks out a set of her most plain and rugged linens. Scanning the shoes in the closet—her mother had a point—all her sandals were stylish with beads and bright colors. They probably wouldn't last through a short hike, let alone the unknown. In the back of her closet, she spies a shoebox and remembers the hiking sandals given to her for her birthday a couple of years ago. After removing the box from the shelf, dust flies into the air that makes her sneeze. Once she pulls the brown, plain sandals with strong straps and thick soles out of the box, she knows they are just right.

After breakfast, Mikita enters the meditation room where her father is already shuffling around. He's cleaning all the papers off the desk and opens the book he took off-the-shelf yesterday. He focuses on a section in one of the middle pages.

When he notices Mikita, he looks up and smiles.

"Good morning, father. I guess I'm ready to get started."

"Ah, let me see. I think I've found what I was looking for." He returns to the book and flips through a few pages before tapping a page with his finger. "Yes, here it is." He stands cradling the opened book with one arm. With his free hand, he motions toward the back deck. "Shall we proceed outside?"

Mikita turns and notices he had already placed two mats on the deck. The sun is rising just above the horizon, and its shine is creeping to the middle of the yard. She looks at him before walking to the screen door. Her father follows behind and they step outside. After sitting down cross-legged on the mats, he places the book in front of them and they sit quietly. She can smell the moisture of the early morning lingering in the air, and she shifts her body weight, so it's centered between her hip bones.

Kitchwan picks up the book and points to a passage in the text. "Let's try this before the meditation. Just read the text and tell me what you feel."

Mikita draws in a breath that comes out with a sigh as she grasps the book.

Her father gently places his hand on her arm to stall handing off the book. "Just relax and enjoy reading it. There are no right or wrong answers here. No reason to analyze anything."

Mikita nods and places the book on her lap. She reads out loud, "*We are part of something far larger than ourselves, yet we play a unique role in the interconnection of all things. If we think of consciousness as growing to higher and higher levels of awareness beyond ourselves, we see an evolution in having a wider and wider perspective of the world around us.*"

She pauses before reading on. "*This process is what binds us to each other and everything else we encounter. It creates a mechanism for a spiritual base and a higher understanding of ourselves.*"

"Okay, how does that make you feel?" asks Kitchwan.

She takes a moment. "Calm and peaceful."

"Good. What else?"

This time, she scans for sensations inside her body to express deeper feelings. "I feel something inside my chest, around my heart."

Her father continues to give her encouragement. "Excellent, go on."

"It's like a ring around my heart or something that is surrounding it."

"Good. Now inside that ring?"

Mikita's eyes squinch as she tries to focus further on the sensation. "There is nothing inside; it's well, hollow."

"Very good. We will meditate now. Focus on the calm and the feeling surrounding your heart. Continue focusing on the feelings as you allow your thoughts to pass. At the same time, I will meditate on phrases for your successful journey. When you are ready, start on the path to the east."

She turns to her father and asks, "How will I know when I'm ready?"

Kitchwan turns to his daughter. "Don't worry. You will know. Trust yourself and follow the intuition inside of you. Just don't forget to see your mother and get the backpack she has prepared for your journey."

Despite being unsure of everything that got her to this point, Mikita turns toward the forest that surrounds the back of the house. Then she sits tall and raises her chin a bit before closing her eyes. At first, her thoughts scatter in a way that makes her uncomfortable. Under the darkness of her eyelids, she allows the thoughts to pass and focuses on her calm center alongside the sensation in her chest.

As the silence takes over in her mind, tingles rise up her spine. Grounded in her calm center keeps the confusion and fear from becoming overwhelming. She continues to focus on the sensation in her chest. Suddenly, the tingling energy moves up her spine into her heart. It fills the inside of the circle until it feels the same as in her dream when she looked at the flower bud.

Eventually, a similar but more subtle tingling sensation continues to travel to her head through the very top. Once this happens, her eyes spontaneously pop open and they take in everything around her. The sun has risen so its streams encase most of the yard. She sees how the grass and ground cover are especially green and lush. The tall trees tower upward and their green leaves contrast with the bright blue sky. The leaves move in waves of perfect harmony as they rustle against one another in each passing breeze. As they do, the sunlight reflects off their surface, making them twinkle in delight.

She enjoys everything for a few moments before turning towards her father who is still in meditation. "I am ready to go now," she whispers.

He opens his eyes, looks at her, and smiles, "Be well. Many blessings on your journey. Trust in the way of things. Trust in the interconnection of all things and the process of consciousness. Let me know when you return."

Beauty and Balance

Mikita looks to the steps on the deck, thinking she can walk directly from there toward the east. But she remembers her father's previous instructions and turns to walk into the house to find her mother.

She passes through the living area and into the kitchen. Her mother is using a dishcloth to wipe breakfast crumbs off the counter.

"Hello Mama. Father said you have prepared a backpack for me."

Her mother stops what she is doing and turns to Mikita. "Hello Mikita. How are you? Doing well?"

With a slight nod she replies, "Yes, I'm okay."

"That's good to hear. Yes, I have it right here." Caresse walks over to the entryway and picks up a brown, rugged, and well-worn backpack.

Mikita didn't notice it sitting right next to her. She accepts the backpack from her mother, not sure if she should inspect what is inside.

Caresse says with grace, "It has things you might want. You know, like a blanket, warm sweater, some cashews and hearty granola, and, of course, bottles of water."

Mikita looks up, making eye contact with her mother.

In response to the eye contact, her mother smiles and clasps her hands together. "Have a good exploratory! You will be fine."

"Thank you." Mikita walks out of the kitchen, then stops. "Mama, is there anything else I should take?"

"Good question…" Caresse looks at Mikita for a moment before picking up an elastic hair tie and gauzy scarf off the kitchen counter. "Take these, they may come in handy."

Mikita takes the items and gives them an inspection. "They aren't very pretty."

"No, but you may be happy to have them on hand."

"Of course. Thank you again. I'm grateful for the gift." Mikita places the hair tie and scarf safely in an outside pocket of the backpack. She slides the arm straps up to her shoulders, then leans into her mother and hugs her deeply.

"I will be here when you return," says Caresse.

"Bye Mama." Mikita walks out of the kitchen.

After a few steps outside, Mikita looks at the house and considers running back to its shelter and comfort, but she scans the surrounding trees that thicken into a forest until she is facing east. Once she takes a few more steps, she spies a small opening in the trees and wonders, "*Is that a path? I've never noticed a path there before.*"

In the opening, she finds a clear path made of rustic wooden planks. The short planks are laid next to one another on the ground. With nothing to lose, she takes the first step on the wooden planks and minutes later finds herself walking through the lush forest of tall trees and dense foliage. The sun is no longer in direct view, so she trusts the direction of the path.

Eventually, the wooden planks end to reveal a well-worn dirt trail. With her toes on the edge of the transition from wood to dirt, Mikita stops for a moment. In the stillness, she listens to the noises of the forest. There are leaves swishing high in the sky, birds chirping from their branches, and insects making buzzing sounds from secret hiding places. She takes off her backpack to retrieve a bottle of water and quenches the thirst in her throat. After she returns the bottle to her backpack and places the backpack on her back, she looks down the dirt trail. It continues for as far as her eye can see.

"It's still early in the day, I'll continue down the path and see where it takes me," she thinks.

The dirt path holds out for a good part of the morning, and Mikita notices a patch of sunlight ahead. Then the sunlight reveals what looks like an opening in the forest. She notices her pace picking up as the opening grows closer and closer. Reaching the opening, her eyes adjust to strong sunlight and the scene of knee-high yellow grass sprawling across the land strikes her. She draws in a quick breath then says out loud, "How beautiful!"

She jogs along the trail a short way and stops to take in the new world. The sun warms her face and body. Dry air flowing along a slight breeze replaces the moist, still air of the forest bottom. In the breeze are smells of crispy grass and dusty earth, while the yellow grass crinkles as the blades brush one another. In the distance, there are patches of green grass with sparsely spaced trees. The trees aren't the same as the towering trees of the forest. They are much shorter, and the branches jut out quickly in elongated tuffs that display small leaves.

She thinks, "*This must be the grasslands.*"

After adjusting her backpack so it's more comfortable, she treks along, still soaking in the environment. Suddenly, she hears the grass rustle and crunch in the distance. She looks behind her and remembers a time she overheard Mr. Reedy and another man talk about lions who live in the grasslands while they were standing outside of the Community Center. The man she didn't know was younger than Mr. Reedy and was wearing a red ball cap with his brown hair sticking out of the sides.

"Really, you were in the grasslands?" asked Mr. Reedy.

"Yeah. I only saw them once, but boy, I tell you, those lions are something. They are like huge versions of the cats that hunt mice on the farm. As big as three or four men."

"That's hard to believe."

The man in the ball cap nodded twice. "I know. I wouldn't have believed it if I hadn't seen them myself. To boot, the guide said they hunt and stalk like most cats. They crouch down and blend in with the grass so they can sneak up on you. By the time you know what's happening, it's too late."

Mikita tries to shake off the memory and tells herself the stories about the fierceness of the lions are just myths, but her heart is already pounding in her chest. She kneels close to the ground, trying to hide. Her eyes focus on the dirt so she can listen better with her ears, and she hears another rustle. After looking further down the path where the noise seemed to come from, she tenses and holds her breath.

An antelope is standing on the path. The antelope stays frozen while staring at her, and Mikita stares back as she slowly stands up from her crouch. The antelope is beautiful, golden-brown with black accents on its face, and a black rugged stripe down its side. Its legs are extremely thin. She never realized how such strong legs could be so delicate.

They stare at each other for a moment, Mikita becoming completely still and the antelope flicking its small tail back and forth. The silence is broken when the antelope speaks to her, "Hello, I'm Zella."

Mikita leans her body back and tilts her head. "Zella?"

"Yes. What is your name?"

Mikita looks around. "My name is Mikita."

Zella trots in place on her small hooves. "Mikita, are you afraid?"

"I am worried about lions."

"The lions are mighty. But don't worry, you can be at peace that the lions are not hunting here."

Mikita watches as Zella raises her nose in the breeze and sniffs for any signs of danger. "Oh, I see." She walks down the path and says, "I am on an exploratory."

"Yes, you're a visitor in the grasslands." Zella turns over her shoulder and calls, "Hey everyone, come meet Mikita."

In moments, a small herd of antelope surround her on the path and follow alongside. Their greetings fill the air with uplifting chatter. She can make out one voice with a softer tone than Zella saying, "Greetings Mikita, we're so glad you're visiting."

Then she can hear another with a grumbly deep voice. "So nice to meet you!"

One of the youngest of the herd jumps straight-up in air as if all four of its legs were made of bouncy springs. Its jumps extend into leaps as it crosses in front of Mikita, then around her side. She can't help but smile and giggle.

In rhythm with its unique leaps, the young antelope says, "Hello Mikita! That's a very pretty name. My name is Pronk."

"Hello Pronk, very nice to meet you," she says.

Again, Zella addresses the herd. "Mikita is on an exploratory. We are going to escort her across the grasslands. She is worried about the lions."

At the word lions, the herd abruptly stops, and their small tails flick back and forth. Some of them smell the air, and others turn to look around them in every direction while talking amongst themselves.

Pronk cranes his head to look above the grass and says, "Lions, where? Where?"

"No, there are no lions here. It's just that our new friend Mikita worries about the lions. We're going to keep her company." Zella soothes Pronk.

"Whew! Okay," says Pronk.

The herd relaxes too, and in unison they all return to walking the path.

Pronk does a few more leaps. "Yay! We will travel with our new friend today."

The conversation falls silent, and they continue along until they come upon a small patch of green grass with a single tree. Some antelopes from the herd are already grazing and seeking the shade to shelter them from the sun.

Zella says, "We will stop, graze and take a break."

At the thought of food, Mikita's stomach rumbles. "Sounds good. I'm starving. And now I think of it, thirsty too."

Mikita walks over to the tree and opens the backpack. The blanket is perfect for a picnic lunch. She gets comfortable before taking out the granola, and the partially finished water bottle. The antelope go about their business, grazing around, taking turns looking for any activity, and surveying the air.

Mikita's stomach becomes full and warm, so she packs up the remaining granola. She remembers the hair tie and scarf in the pocket on the outside of the bag. While digging into the pocket she thinks, "*Thank you, Mama, for the hair tie.*"

With her long hair pulled back, the breeze caresses her neck and Mikita feels cooler. She examines the long, white, gauzy scarf and gets an idea. She takes the scarf and carefully sprinkles it with water until it's damp. Then she wraps the damp scarf around her neck and ties it at the front.

The herd has scatted, and Zella makes her way to the trail. She says, "Okay, let's continue traveling."

Mikita rises, folds the blanket, and packs everything into her bag. She walks alongside Zella. "Thank you for escorting me through the grasslands. I hate the thought of the lions."

Zella looks at Mikita as they walk. "Hate? Hate is overwhelming."

"Well, yes, hate. Don't you hate the lions? They prey upon the antelope."

"That they do. When we encounter lions on the prowl, we experience fear and a host of other things that tell us to run, but those experiences aren't about hate. If the lions didn't have prey to hunt and eat, they wouldn't survive. At the same time, if wasn't for the lion, the herd would be so large the land couldn't sustain all of us and some would slowly starve or die of thirst."

Thinking about Pronk, Mikita asks, "So, you don't hate them even when they take your young?"

After a few more steps, Zella continues speaking. "That is the way of things. Everything in nature has a balance. Look around you, what do you see?"

"That sounds like a question my father would ask." Mikita looks around her and how she felt when she first entered the grasslands fill her insides. "I don't know. I see beauty, I guess."

Zella nods and snorts through her nostrils. "Yes, beauty and balance. Each life, despite its uniqueness, simply can't do without the other living things. Everything is interconnected. Do you get it now?"

"Sort of."

With a joyous laugh, Zella says, "We don't think about it so much. We just know that it *is*. In time you will understand. It isn't far to the end of the grasslands."

Mikita keeps walking as Zella prances off toward the rest of the herd. The path takes a slight bend and reveals a large area of green grass with many trees.

As they approach the grassy area, Mikita sees that in between two of the trees are rocks and eventually deep blue water. She also hears a soft crashing sound that gets louder the further they travel down the trail. At the edge of the grassy area, the herd clusters.

Zella faces Mikita. "This is the end of the grasslands. We can't escort you any further."

Mikita looks at all the antelope, “Thank you my new friends! I am so happy to have met you.”

Pronk leaps out. “You’re welcome. This is so cool. I haven’t been this close to the end of the grasslands.” He leaps a few more times. “Good luck!”

The rest of the herd responds likewise in a rise of joyous comments. Zella turns her head toward the opening with the blue water then makes eye contact with Mikita. “Continue on your exploratory. Be well and good luck.”

Mikita walks over to her new antelope friend, leans over, and gives her a light hug. “Thank you,” she says.

After entering a small way into the grassy area, Mikita notices the herd turning back towards the heart of the grasslands. The beloved breeze flows by and she finds herself alone again.

Interconnection

Following the path, the rhythmic crashing sound gets louder and louder. Mikita makes it to the opening and sees the waves rolling across the water. They raise, and then tumble over themselves as they meet the shore with a rumble. The musty smell of saltwater spray is strong. Over and over, the waves come—raising, tumbling, rumbling, then splashing the surrounding ground. Wind swirls in different directions inside the bay.

She attempts to get her bearings as quickly as possible by scanning the area. Gray, mossy boulders surround her on both sides. On one side, they continue down a slope into the water. On the other side, the path curves around the boulders until they end, revealing a calm shoreline. She feels tiny while walking around the tall and wide boulders. To help navigate around the curve, she places her hand on one of them. "*This must be the sea,*" she thinks.

Mikita makes it past the rugged terrain and heads down the slope that leads to the shoreline. The wind is steadily increasing and whips all around her. The crashing of the waves comes quicker and quicker. She looks at the sky and notices dark clouds approaching. Similar to the waves, they roll tumbling below themselves but with nothing to crash into they reach out with growing fingers headed toward the ground. She sees rain streaking from the clouds on the horizon.

Again, she scans the area around her and continues moving quickly down the slope, hoping it leads to a sheltered area. The wind has become relentless, occasionally making it difficult to keep her footing, and the rapid crashing of the waves has become so loud they make it difficult to concentrate. A darkness surrounds her as the clouds move in, covering the sun.

Lightning streaks across the sky, and Mikita jumps as the distinct rumble of thunder moves across the ground. She does her best to increase her pace as the lighting increases. In distinct spurts, the lightning flashes with brilliance, spreading out in branch after branch, exploding with energy. It reflects off the water, enhancing the crest of each rolling wave. In the light, she looks down the trail, but she can't tell where it leads. A sprinkle of rain sprays the side of her face. She contemplates returning to the grasslands. But she would be on her own for the night.

Mikita runs down the path. The sprinkle of rain progresses to a steady rain and with a gush, a downpour. She continues to run until the path appears to end where the protected shoreline meets with the water. Out of breath, her mind asks, "*What? What is happening?*"

She gets a little closer to the water and waits for the next streak of lighting to alleviate her disbelief about what she is seeing. The lightning flashes, and it's clear the path leads into the sea. The rain rolls down her face and drips off her chin. With the wind swirling, waves crashing, lighting streaking, thunder rumbling, rain pounding all around her, she falls to her knees, clenches her hands, looks up, and yells, "What now? What do I do?"

Mikita attempts to regain her breath and lowers her head. She closes her eyes and searches for her confident center. Despite the storm surrounding her, soon she can take a deep breath and exhale it slowly. She remembers her father telling her she will head east to the grasslands and beyond; for her to trust herself and the intuition inside of her, followed by his last words about trusting in the way of things. A memory follows about Zella explaining how the lion prey upon the antelope is part of the way of things, and the antelope don't think about it so much.

Zella's joyous laughter echoes in her mind, and Mikita opens her eyes thinking, "*Head east. Trust. Don't think about it so much.*" She stands and focuses on a point on the other side of the bay and slowly follows the path as it leads into the sea. Without a thought, she continues her steps until the water reaches above her knees, then she dives into its depths.

Underneath the surface of the water, she continues to dive deeper and finds shelter from the storm. She looks sideways over her shoulder and can see waves crashing above her on the surface. Somehow, she is comfortable under the water, and when she contemplates how it's possible, she reminds herself to trust and not to think about it so much.

Her backpack is causing resistance while moving through the water, so she tightens the arm straps as much as possible. Her hiking sandals stay firm on her feet, but the white gauzy scarf loosens and eventually comes off her neck, drifting behind her in the water currents. She uses her arms to dive deeper down until she can see the seafloor.

The array of strange plant life causes her to stop and transfix on the view. Some of it sways with the currents but others don't give way. It's all so colorful.

Some of them are golden brown, some green, and others are red. When she gets a little closer, the plants grow upward in a rigid form. The tall ones resemble a tree with bare branches, and the short ones a bush without foliage. Their surfaces are textured with bumps or nooks and crannies. Then it connects in her mind. This isn't plant life—it's coral. "*This is a coral reef! How incredible!*"

Mikita becomes immersed in the reef. The coral gets very dense, and an array of fish swim around and above the coral. Soon they are swimming around her too. What looks like a large, flat, fleshy snake emerges from in between firmly planted coral and debris. The rim of its bright white eyes and snaggled teeth protrude from the blackness of its skin. "*That looks like an eel. It's probably better to leave that alone.*" And she keeps swimming.

Soon, she notices a group of small silver and white fish in a school shaped like an oval. They dart in one direction, then another. With each turn in direction, what light there is beneath the water reflects off their sides while they all stay in complete synchronicity together. They dive around the arm of a coral, staying in the school and in synch with each other.

She swims fast to catch up with the little fish. "Hello there!"

The school of fish pays her no mind and continues with their random yet highly coordinated dance.

Mikita gives it another try. "I say, hello there!"

This time they respond. She can hear different voices but similar to their swimming, they respond in unison. "Hello."

"My name is Mikita, and I have traveled from another land. How do you-all do that? I mean swim like that?"

Just like before, the fish reply together, "Swim like what? We all swim all the time!" They dart the other direction, then dart back, finishing by gathering in a swirl formation in front of Mikita.

"How do you swim together in a school? You-all move together in unison without a set plan. It's beautiful, really."

"Oh, that. There are lots of reasons: where the others are, what the water currents are doing, what's around us. We can't say, we don't think about it much or plan it or anything."

"Really?" asks Mikita.

"Well, yes. We become part of the beauty and balance that makes-up the rhythm of nature. The interconnection of all that is around us. That is the way of things." After that statement, the sound of each fish in the school is distinct as they joyously laugh and dart in one direction, then the other, before zipping around a couple of large coral.

Mikita floats a minute while staring where the school disappeared. She redirects her course to continue to swim across the bay. As she gets started, she does a somersault in the water and happily giggles. She swims and the hearty coral reef becomes a little sparser. Then she comes across a circular coral grounded on the sandy floor. It's an arm's length across with an empty center. As she gets closer, she sees that the coral is made of a series of bumps and broken white shells are resting on the seafloor in the middle. She tilts her head and inspects the strange sight.

A large fish approaches the coral ring. The fish is brilliant shades of teal blue covered with orange spots, has yellow fins protruding from each side next to its gills, and a white underbelly. The fish has a shell in its mouth, and he drops it in the middle of the ring. The fish looks up at her and says, "Hey, there! What are you doing?"

"Hello, I am on an exploratory, visiting from another land," she replies.

The fish's body slightly wriggles and its fins oscillate to stabilize itself in the water. "Are you hungry? Would you like a clam to eat?"

"Thank you, but I don't eat clams." Mikita shifts her body weight and pulls her arms close to her, so she sinks down to the seafloor. She gets to eye level and sees that fish's eyes are accented by rings of orange. It also has a few blunt teeth protruding from the top and bottom lips. "My name is Mikita. What is your name?"

"Name?"

"Why, yes. What do I call you?"

"You can call me Tusky."

Mikita bows her head toward Tusky. "It's good to meet you."

He turns and extends his front fin in her direction while saying, "Sure, likewise."

With a smile, Mikita leans over to shake his fin, using her thumb and a couple of fingers.

He returns to the coral ring and grabs the shell with his mouth. In his mouth, the shell sits nicely between his protruding teeth. The shell is closed, but she figures there is a clam tucked inside. He takes his powerful head and thrusts it to the side, so the clam flies out of his mouth and crashes against the coral. He picks the clam up again, but this time it slips from his mouth—flipping and sinking slowly to the bottom.

"What are you doing?" she asks.

Tusky pauses and replies, "I'm breaking open this clam to eat. Clams are my favorite food." Then he continues to pick up the clam. By using the same motion, he thrusts the clam into the coral. C*link.* The shell is still intact, so he picks it up again and it slips out of his mouth.

Mikita can't help but ask, "Can I try it?"

"Of course."

She picks up the clam in her hand and tries throwing it like a toy ball against the coral. Given the unexpected resistance of the water, the clam slides down the side of the coral.

"No, no. Flick it close to the coral. Put some muscle into it. Flick it so it hits this bump here." Tusky instructs as he does a sideways nod toward a specific bump in the coral.

"Okay." She picks up the claim and flicks it with all her strength using a sidearm throw. It hits the coral with a tiny, *clink.* During the throw, a streak of pain moved through her shoulder, so she rubs it with the other hand.

Tusky heartily laughs. "Well, it takes practice. See, it's like this." He picks up the clam and flicks it against the bump in the coral. C*link!* He does it again. *Clink!* A crack opens in the shell, and tiny pieces fly off, spiraling down to land by other pieces of shell. He picks it up and repeats the motion. C*link.* This time the shell breaks apart, and he quickly slurps up the clam. "Ahhh, yummm. That was good."

"That's a lot of effort for a little bit of food," says Mikita.

Tusky looks at her. "That's a curious thing to say."

"Do you really think so?"

"Why, yes. Let me put it this way, do I appear thin?" asks Tusky.

"No, you're very muscular."

"Malnourished?"

"Of course not, you're quite handsome," she says with a slight blush, and she raises her hand to cover the coy smile on her face.

"So, everything is well, all is in balance. I get what I need from the work it takes to open the clams just as much as I do from eating them. Many fish like me have become very good at breaking the clams open. That is the way of things."

"I'm starting to get it," says Mikita.

With more laughter he says, "I'm glad. I never really thought about it before now. Time for me to seek another clam. Well wishes on the rest of your travels, Mikita!"

"Thank you for everything, Tusky."

Tusky turns and takes off to parts where he looks for clams in the sand and rubble. Mikita swims upward before turning toward the other side of the bay. "*Onward! Surely, I can't stay in the sea forever,*" she thinks.

The reef gets sparser until it gives way to a sandy bottom. It isn't long until the seafloor slopes upward. Mikita can vaguely see the other side of the bay and diligently swims to a good spot to get on shore. The slope continues in an upward direction, and the water gets shallow. Eventually, she stands and walks to the stony beach.

Water drips off her clothes and drains from her backpack as she hikes onto dry land. The storm has passed, and late day sunlight has returned. She looks to the horizon, and the clouds are rumbling on their way. The angle of the sunshine through the rain creates a distinct rainbow that streaks across the sky, each end meeting the land far in the distance. In its magnificence, the rainbow shows off all its colors as they blend into one another.

Mikita reaches the beach, where she heads for small boulders that lay between the rocky sand and forest. There are prickly trees that look like typical evergreen trees, but these are uniformly thin and bare at the bottom, then branch out with needles high up the trunk. One of the smaller trees has a low branch which is perfect. She opens the backpack and removes the soggy blanket to hang and dry in the breeze coming off the sea. While adjusting the blanket so it's spread out evenly across the limb, she spies the path leading into the forest. Sighing relief, she says out loud, "Thank goodness. I've found my way."

Then she removes the other items from the backpack and finds that her mother packed the sweater in a sealed plastic bag. Holding-up the bag, she examines it, and the sweater is dry. Once again, she sends a silent wish of gratitude to her mother. She removes the sweater, places the items left in the backpack into the plastic bag, and returns to hang the backpack the same as the blanket.

Mikita sits on a small boulder to dry off before she warms herself with the sweater. While resting her tired body, she realizes her stomach is terribly empty. She enjoys the scenery of the beach, soft sounds of the surf and the rainbow in the distance as she nibbles on the cashews and opens a new water bottle. As time passes, the colors of the rainbow fade, and she notices the sun is getting low in the sky. There doesn't seem to be much shelter on the beach for the night, so she starts hiking the trail.

Uniqueness

The path quickly takes her into a forest. Dried needles that have shed from the trees cover the ground. It has a distinct earthy and strong foliage smell that is satisfying as it fills her nostrils. Smaller trees with leaves start to appear and she can hear flowing water. She comes closer to the sound and sees a stream.

In the stream, water glides over small rocks. The coating of water brightens the rocks alongside years of being polished by the action within the stream. Her journey follows the stream and progresses on a slight incline. She takes care in her steps but can't seem to take her eyes off the moving water. It burbles along without a care in the world.

Mikita allows herself to stay enchanted until the trail curves away from the stream. She continues on, still feeling calm and peaceful while humming a tune. Soon her hike meets a small pond surrounded by grass with a few small streams headed to nearby leafy trees. She explores the pond with her eyes, and there are ripples on top of the calm water. Intently watching the motion, she sees an animal swimming with its head poking out of the water.

Mikita and the animal come close to one another as she follows the edge of the pond. While being distracted by the animal, she misses a dried-up branch on the dirt path. As her step lands on the dried branch, its little limbs, along with the leaves, crack and crinkle. The noise reverberates over the silent pond while she stumbles. The animal reacts to the noise by flipping its large tail upward and raising its head; then the tail and head make a splash as it retreats to underneath the surface.

Mikita quickly regains her balance. While pulling out the twigs and dried leaves stuck in her sandal, she hears a deep voice, "Are you alright? Sorry about the splash, you startled me." After a momentary pause with a hearty chuckle he says, "Well, actually I enjoy giving others a good splash!"

Mikita looks up and smiles. "Yes, I'm fine. I didn't mean to startle you. You are an excellent swimmer. Are you a beaver?"

"Yes, I am Castor."

"Hello, I'm Mikita. I am on a journey, exploring."

"Oh, I see. It's been a long time since anyone has followed the path this far."

"I believe it, it's been an adventure," says Mikita.

"Well, welcome to the woodlands!"

"Thank you. Your forest is enchanting."

"The trail follows the pond all the way to my lodge. Walk with me while I swim along."

"To your lodge?"

"Yes, my home."

"I would be happy too," says Mikita.

Castor glides forward in the water, and she continues walking. She thinks a minute and asks, "Is it true you build dams?"

"Why yes, the dams I built made this pond. Well, me and the family built, that is. We also made the canals so we can swim closer to the trees."

"That's amazing, and did you say family?"

"Yes, family. There is the Missus, then we have two kits, you know, beavers born this year, and one yearling."

"How nice! And you built the lodge where you all live?"

"You bet yah! It's a fine lodge too. It's not far," replies Castor.

"I can't wait to see it."

They round a small corner and Mikita can see the lodge. It's dome-shaped and looks like a hut made of branches and earth. Yellow and pink colors fill the sky as the sun lowers closer to sunset. She heartily yawns, exhausted from such a long and eventful day.

"Say, would you like to stay at my lodge tonight?" Castor chuckles. "Well, you're too big to fit inside so you would have to sleep on top of it, but it would be warm and dry."

Enthusiastic, Mikita replies, "Yes, that would be fantastic, but is it strong enough to hold me?"

"Oh yes, it will hold you. It can withstand any bear who tries to break through its walls. They are much bigger and heavier than you."

Mikita's voice escalates to a high pitch. "Bears? Really? Are there really bears around here?"

"There are bears in the woodlands, but it's rare that they come around the lodge. With little chance of success in finding a good meal, it's not enticing."

"Oh, okay. That sounds reassuring."

As they approach the lodge, Mikita sees it's made of branches stripped bare of their limbs and bark that are cemented in a patchwork with dried grasses and earth. Its base impressively sits in the water along the side of the pond. She walks toward the lodge and

Castor climbs out of the water onto the side of the structure. For the first time, Mikita can see he is covered by course, brown fur and his dark tail is large, flat, and wide. At the end, his tail rounds in a shape like a boat paddle. His feet are also darker, and his paws look almost like fins. Still hesitant to get on top of the lodge, she waits for Castor.

Castor is keen to her hesitation and says, "Come on up."

"And you're sure your family won't mind visitors?"

"Well, no. We like company. We have all kinds of critters stay in the lodge, a pair of muskrats, and occasionally, a frog or two stays with us. Especially in the colder months."

"Wow, that's interesting." She gently crawls up the lodge, and it's strong and sturdy. At a spot near the top, she sits cross-legged facing Castor.

"Sure. Plus, there are so many visitors that come to the pond," says Castor.

"Yes, I noticed all the birds enjoying the water."

"Maybe tomorrow you can stop and see my friend Ribbon. He raises tadpoles safely on the other side of the pond. He would like to meet you."

"Okay, I will keep an eye out for him… Can I ask you a question?"

"Of course."

"How do you get the earth cemented in between the tree branches to make your home?"

"Well, we gather it from the bottom of the pond, put it where we want to strengthen the hut, and it dries firm. Want to see?"

"I think that would be exciting," says Mikita.

Castor dives into the water, sending ripples across the surface of the pond. A short time later he resurfaces in the same place with mud piled in his arms, so it's tucked next to his chest. He climbs rather gracefully up the side of the lodge. "Here is a cranny that could use reinforcement." Then he dumps mud into a small hole, and it settles into the cracks. "This is also how we build our dams."

"Impressive! It reminds me of my friend Tusky. He's a very skilled fish. He breaks open clam shells against the coral."

"You have been on an adventure," says Castor.

"Indeed." Then Mikita asks, "Have beavers always known how to construct dams, and lodges?"

Castor looks at her inquisitively before saying, "I don't know for sure. I guess I haven't thought about it so much. It's just we do what we do. All I can say for sure is we all have our own talents, even amongst us beavers. The Missus is much better at creating canals than me, and I build master dams, so we work well together. Talents unique to each of us, yet all things are interconnected. That is the way of things."

The colors in the sky have deepened to pink and orange. Mikita nods at him and covers a fresh yawn with her hand.

"Well, it's time for you to rest now. You'll be safe here unless a bear pays a random visit."

She tries to keep her voice level. "Are you kidding?"

Castor falls back on his haunches exposing his belly and his chuckle turns into full-blown laughter. "Don't worry. I do most of my work at night and will slap my tail on the water at the sign of any danger."

"You work through the night?"

"Yes, for the most part, and I should get started. The Missus will be out soon to join me." Just as he finishes his sentence, another beaver pops its head out of the water.

Castor looks at the other beaver. "Hello dear. This is Mikita. She is traveling through and is going to sleep on the lodge tonight." He turns back to Mikita and gestures. "Mikita, this is the Missus."

"Welcome, Mikita. I'm Missy." With a smile and cheerful tone, she says, "Castor likes to be funny and call me *the Missus*. Glad you will stay with us; we like visitors. We'll keep an eye out for you as you sleep."

"Thank you. I appreciate the place to stay and the comfort that both of you are my gracious hosts." Mikita buttons her sweater all the way to the top and opens her backpack.

Castor looks at Missy and says, "Well, we should get started. I can hear a trickle of water flowing across the larger dam. Where are the kits and the yearling? Are they coming out with us for a while?"

"Here they come," says Missy.

Castor nods at her and turns toward Mikita, "Have a good night." Then he dives off the lodge into the water.

Both Castor and Missy greet one another by rubbing faces and touching noses. As soon as the two kits see Castor, they squeal and grunt with delight. They swim over to him, rub his face, and climb on him.

"Ahhh, you're pushing me under!" Castor jokes. He continues with the act and sinks his head underwater.

The kits squeal again until he comes back to the surface. He laughs and lets them climb on him until he says, "All right. You just saw me this afternoon."

The yearling stays close to Missy, observing the child-like fun. Castor looks at them and says, "Let's get a move on." They all swim together on the surface until one-by-one the family disappears under the water.

"What a day," whispers Mikita. She takes the blanket and stretches it out on the lodge. She lies on one side of the blanket and pulls the other side over her like a sleeping bag. As a last touch, the backpack makes a pretty good pillow. She nestles into her makeshift bed and finds her sleeping arrangement more comfortable than expected.

The sun has almost disappeared, and the last streaks of bright orange light meet with the horizon. Stars appear in the sky, and Mikita lies on her back watching them rise while listening to the crickets, bullfrogs, and the surrounding night sounds. She can pick out one especially loud bullfrog, *Ribb-onnon, Ribb-ib-onn* and lightheartedly thinks, "*I wonder if that is Castor's friend Ribbon.*"

Chasing the sun, a brilliant full moon appears on the other side of the horizon. Soon stars fill the night sky, and she can't remember seeing so many. They are bright and bold, shining as they always do, along with the dazzling moon. With a sense of the sun, moon and stars traveling around her while lying on the dome-shaped hut in the wilderness, she drifts off into a restful and deep sleep.

Mikita wakes to the sound of splashing water. Abruptly sitting, she surveys the scene around the lodge.

Water droplets reach high in the air and land on her face. Castor is in the pond by the hut, repeatedly slapping his tail and diving into the pond.

"What is it? Is there danger? Is there a bear?" she exclaims.

Castor comes to the surface and heartily chuckles. "I like you, Mikita."

"Gee, thanks," she says and wipes the water from her face. "I like you too, even though you're such a jokester."

"Well, it's time to get-up. The sun has fully risen!"

"Okay, I'm up. I'm awake." Warm now, she pulls the blanket off her legs and unbuttons the top of her sweater.

"Did you sleep well?" asks Castor.

"Yes, very well. Thanks. I trust you had a productive night."

"I did, but I have a couple of things to finish. I'll be back to say goodbye."

"Sounds good. I will get something to eat and get ready to return on my exploratory."

Just when Mikita finishes getting ready and climbs off of the lodge, Castor and Missy appear in the water. They swim to where the path is closest to the edge of the pond.

"I'm most grateful for the refuge last night. I enjoyed sleeping under the stars," says Mikita.

"You are welcome! We're glad you were comfortable," says Castro.

"You are welcome back anytime." Missy adds.

"Goodbye and good luck on the rest of your travels," says Castro.

"Thank you!" After a wave and a few steps, Mikita turns and leaves the beaver family behind.

•

Wider Perspective

The trail meanders along the edge of the beaver pond. The sun has risen and finds its way deep into the woodlands. There is sunlight shining through the moist air and the birds have ended their morning songs. For no particular reason, Mikita has a sense that she will return home soon. She trusts the intuition and does her best to soak in everything around her to become enchanted by the forest.

The hike peacefully continues, and Mikita reaches the other side of the pond. Her ears perk up when she hears a familiar call, "*Ribb-onn…*"

She stops and scans the edge of the pond. It comes again, "*Ribb-onn,*" followed by a swishing sound ruminating from the grass in the water. "*It must be Castor's friend, Ribbon.*"

The swishing comes closer, then grass on the edge of the pond moves around. She hones her eyesight on the patch of grass, and says, "Hello. Is that you, Ribbon?"

A huge frog jumps with a high arch and delicately lands next to the edge of the path. With that entrance he says, "Mikita!"

She takes a small step backward. "Yes, it's Mikita. How did you know?"

"Castor visited very early this morning and told me all about you," he replies.

"I should have known. So, you are Ribbon?"

"Of course. I'm happy to meet you."

Mikita sits down close to Ribbon and looks him over. His large brown eyes protrude from his head, and they contrast with his glistening green body. Then there are spots of brown on his back, slowly transitioning to white spots that lead to his underside. "I'm most happy to meet you too."

"I can't stay long because my tadpoles are still in the shallow area where they hatch," he says.

"Can I come and see the tadpoles?"

"No, I'm very protective of the area. I don't want to call attention to those who prey on young tadpole. Its location is mostly a secret."

"I understand." Yet, Mikita looks down and allows her lower lip to protrude a little.

"You know what? I will call a few to the edge of the pond so you can see them; it should be safe."

"All right, I would like that, but just for a moment. I don't want to put them in any danger."

"No, it won't be too risky. Follow me." Ribbon traverses the grass, headed for the pond.

Likewise, Mikita follows him while crawling on her hands and knees.

Ribbon gets to the pond and calls out, "Hey, perimeter poles. Come over quickly and meet Mikita. She's the traveler Castor told us about this morning."

Little voices arise from the water in a mix of phrases and giggles. Mikita can single out some of the voices. One tadpole says, "It's the Mikita person!"

Followed by another who says, "We have a visitor."

Then one exclaims, "This is fun!"

At the edge of the pond next to Ribbon, Mikita sees the little tadpoles swimming around one another.

They have gigantic heads with long tails and are very cute. She can't help but lean closely to the water and say in a sweet voice, "Hello little ones. So nice to see you."

The tadpoles chatter some more, but Ribbon wastes no time in sending them back to the nesting place. "Okay. Return to your home. I'll be there in a minute."

"They are wonderful!" says Mikita.

"Sure, I guess I haven't thought about it much. I have a brood of them every year."

Mikita sits on her knees. "And you like the beaver pond as a place to raise them?"

"Yes, it's the best. Because of what the beaver family creates, the pond never dries-up and provides an abundance of food for the tadpoles. The grass and vegetation also shelter them until they are ready for deeper water. What more could a doting father ask for?"

"I see," says Mikita with a nod.

"It seems you have grown wise. I assume your travels have helped in this process."

"I'm not so sure about the wise part, but I have learned a lot on my travels. Castor said that you would be happy to meet me, but I think it's me who is happy to have met you."

"I assure you; the feeling is likewise. All things are interconnected. That is the way of things."

"Indeed." Mikita smiles and nods.

"I must return to protecting the tadpoles and nesting grounds now. Take care, Mikita. Best wishes on your exploratory."

"Thank you, Ribbon! Best wishes with your young tadpoles."

Ribbon warmly looks her in the eye then jumps back into the pond. In a similar way, she rises and walks to where she was traveling the path.

The pond ends and the rocky flowing stream returns, but the rocks have increased in size and have more uniform colors than last time. It burbles loudly and keeps Mikita company as she hikes along. The trail inclines and rugged forest returns speckled with large trees that have needle foliage. The sun rises higher in the sky and her trek continues higher up the incline. Her strides have become long and more labored until she runs out of breath. She takes a break, sitting on a fallen tree. It takes some rummaging in her backpack to remove a water bottle for a drink. The day has warmed up, and she removes her sweater and packs it away. Ready to move on, she returns to the trail.

The stream becomes rockier, and the forest abruptly ends where a cliff rises. Mikita admires the formation and notes how moss and foliage grow out of the rock until it becomes so high and inhospitable that it turns into stone. Pretty soon, she must look upward to see to the top. Just like the stream, the cliff becomes rockier with smaller cliffs along its face. Countless years of slow shifting and exposure to weather elements have marred the wall of the cliff. When she turns to look at the stream, the trail has moved away from its bank and there is a sharp slope between her and the water.

It becomes difficult to see where the path leads as the cliff rises high above the ground and the slope on the riverside steepens, reminding her of a valley. She has come too far not to make a full investigation, so she walks along, nonetheless. The incline steepens, and the river escalates to becoming a mature rapid. Water crashing over the rocks fills the air with the sounds of tumbling whitewater, and spray from the rapids carries a musky smell of leaves and dirt.

Mikita freezes in place. The trail heads toward the cliff then narrows into a single point where it meets the stone wall. She searches for a clue about how to proceed by scanning the face of the cliff and the landscape by the flowing river. "*Certainly, I'm not going to scale a cliff or mount any rapids.*"

She reflects on the feeling she had earlier this morning that she would return home soon and considers turning around and taking the path back home. That would be an arduous journey, and she doesn't have enough food and water. There must be another way.

She wonders, "*Perhaps I missed something while being enchanted by the stream and the forest. Maybe a split in the path and I took a wrong turn.*" After a pause, she nods and turns around to re-explore the last part of her hike. She takes careful steps back down the incline and over the sounds of the river hears a voice say, "Where are you going?"

Mikita stands straight and instinctively looks to where the voice is coming from. There is a smaller cliff on the side of the rock wall. The sunlight is blinding part of her view, so she uses her hand to shield her eyes. There are a few branches sticking out over the small cliff, but not much else. Still sensing that she's looking in the right area, she shouts, "I am on an exploratory, but the path has ended. I thought I would travel back to see if there was something I missed."

Finally, a head pokes out from the cliff. Even though it's far away, she can make out a head of a bird with striking brown feathers and an intimidating hook-like beak.

"Travel back? But you have reached the end of the trail."

Mikita looks around, and says in a loud voice, "It seems so, but what else am I to do?"

The majestic bird pulls his head back in from the edge and she can hear two voices drifting in the air, but she can't understand what they are saying. Then the bird and another bird both hang their head over the side. The bird with a larger head replies with a softer voice, "What do you think you should do?"

"I need to return home now, back to my village on the other side of the grasslands."

"Very good. You have traveled far on an admirable journey. Give us a moment."

Again, Mikita can hear voices traveling in the air. She waits while shadowing her eyes from the sun to focus on where the birds are located. After what seems like a long time, the larger bird launches itself off the cliff. She had never imagined a bird this large and impressive. As it approaches, her belly quivers. It's covered with silky dark brown feathers, but tan feathers that flash with golden tones accent the back of its head and chest. Its wingspan is breathtaking, more than the height of most men. The underside of its wings has patches of white feathers with the flashy tan-golden feathers at its tips. It glides down to where she is standing without a sound and barely flaps its wings.

Mikita stands still and stares at the bird that she determines must be a golden eagle. The bird with the soft voice meets her gaze and asks, "Can you tell me, what have you learned on your journey?"

She thinks a moment before saying, "That each life has a unique role, but those roles are part of what makes-up the interconnection of all things."

"Yes, what else?" The eagle turns her head and points her ear in Mikita's direction.

"Um, that connection makes-up the beauty and balance of all things around us."

"And you are ready to return home?"

"Yes, I think so," says Mikita.

The eagle opens her wings part-way and curtsies. "My name is Aerie. My companion, Darvell, and I would be happy to take you back home."

"Hello, I'm Mikita. I would be grateful for your help. How would take me home?"

"Oh, don't worry about that, dear," says Aerie. She launches herself and flies back to the cliff.

Mikita wonders what will happen next and shields her eyes like before so she can see upward. One side of both bird's wings stretch out and then they turn sideways before leaving the cliff with wings outstretched while carrying a huge nest in between the two of them. They fly past her and set the nest on the ground.

The eagle with the deeper voice turns back to look at her and says, "Hello Mikita, I'm Darvell." Then he says, "We can take you home, come on, climb into the nest."

Aerie chimes in. "Yes, come on, climb in."

Mikita walks over and inspects the nest made of intricately woven branches reinforced with twigs. As she looks in, she can see a bedding of dried leaves and herbal-smelling plants on the bottom. She finds Darvell and Aerie, gazing at her, nodding their heads.

With little thought, Mikita climbs into the nest and gets comfortable, sitting on the bed of dried foliage. It smells so earthy and green. She pulls in a deep breath to inhale the scent and closes her eyes.

Aerie looks at Darvell and says, "She will do well."

Darvell nods. "Mikita, are you comfortable? The trip may take a little while."

"Yes, I'm ready."

Mikita watches the eagle's large talons tighten around the edges of the nest. Their muscular legs become exposed as they open their massive wings. Slowly lifting the nest, they fly with Aerie positioned near the front and Darvell near the back, so they don't collide with each other. They reach the tops of the trees, and the nest wobbles a bit as they get their wings flapping in rhythm. She grabs a branch on the inside of the nest.

"Don't worry, Mikita, things will smooth out when we get high enough to soar on the air currents," says Darvell.

While not being sure about flying that high, she says, "All right."

They fly higher and Mikita leans over the side so she can see the landscape below. She follows the river with her eyes. Soon the river fans out into the beaver pond. From the high vantage point, she can see all the canals the beavers have dugout. She smiles and wonders where Ribbon's secret nesting grounds are located. The pond widens and there is the beaver lodge where the beaver family is resting for the day. As she looks back, she notes how the stream flows along, the water from the stream makes the beaver pond, and the pond provides life for other habitats in the woodland forest.

Darvell was correct. The flight in the nest has become smooth. The two birds have their wings fully extended, only moving in tiny amounts to keep them and the nest level. They clear the forest that surrounds the beaver pond and catch an air current, so they dive rapidly. Mikita feels her stomach flutter upward and at the same time sink deep into her insides. Again, she grabs a branch on the inside of the nest as the sea where she made her swim comes into full view.

They level out and Mikita thinks of Tusky cracking his clams and the fish dancing in their school. The bright sunlight reflects off the tiny ripples on the surface of the water, but she knows those tiny ripples form together to make waves that crash into the shore. Then, beneath the surface, the water rolls back out to sea, perhaps becoming small ripples again.

The eagles soar upward, flying high in the sky by riding the air current coming off the other side of the bay. They pass the boulders and soon are over the edge of the grasslands. Alongside the green grass by the small trees, she spies what she once thought was a myth. "*Oh, my goodness, there are three lions!*"

Mikita takes in the sight the best that she can from so far away, and Zella was correct—they are mighty. Even in their fight for survival, the lion can't do without the antelope anymore than the antelope can't do without the lion. The beauty and balance of nature and all that is around us. They make up the rhythm of nature that changes and over time evolves. All things change together, establishing an interconnection that can't be easily defined. It's part of the mystery of the universe where each thing has unique talents yet is interconnected with everything else. This is the spiritual base.

She looks ahead and thinks about returning home, with this new perspective she remembers walking through town greeting everyone and the many people who participate in services every week. In particular, she reflects on her connection with Ellen. She remembers how over time, while working with her in one-on-one sessions, Ellen became happier and more confident. Then she started the art gallery that creates more connections by providing space to feature other local artists. She also thinks about how Ellen and Thomas were the happiest she had ever seen them.

Mikita knows now that she looks forward to returning home to continue learning spiritual practices and defining her role in the village. In time, things would change, and she would do things a little differently. She would not strive to become the next spiritual leader. She would work to be a spiritual guide by connecting with individuals in the community, no more, no less. While continuing her spiritual practices as an example, she would also grow to become a more active member of the interconnected community.

Over the heart of the grasslands, the birds encounter another air current born from the warm breezes and dive rapidly. This time Mikita embraces the feeling and instead of grabbing a branch in the nest, she sits upright, takes the hair tie out of her hair, and flings it aside. With the wind flowing all around her and through her long hair, she extends her arms to each side, closes her eyes, tilts her head back, and soars right along with the eagles. The empty part within the ring around her heart becomes so full of warmness she joyously laughs. She embraces how the world around her makes more sense to her than before, and where she wants to be headed is more clear.

At the end of the grasslands, they soar upward one last time as they near the forest that surrounds her house. As they climb in the air, Mikita lets her arms down and her confident center feels strong. A calmness overcomes her as she enjoys how the familiar forest suddenly looks different from the new perspective. They clear the forest, and her house comes into view. She doesn't think much about things like she had in the past, she just knows she is almost home.

Aerie and Darvell glide and tip so they skim the trees and skillfully set the nest in the back yard. Mikita barely notices when the nest settles on the ground. A bit of sadness comes over her as she realizes her exploratory is at an end. Aerie and Darvell look at her, expecting her departure. She climbs out of the nest, getting her footing before turning so she can see both the birds.

"Thank you, that was incredible. I wouldn't have made it home if it wasn't for you two," she says.

Aerie nods deeply. "It was our honor. Not many travelers persist all the way to the end of the path."

"Absolutely. We won't forget you." Darvell agrees.

"It was a very special adventure. I won't forget you or any of the others I met along the way," says Mikita.

"We should go now, dear," says Aerie. She lifts her wing just a little and Mikita steps closer to stroke her wing covered with smooth feathers.

The eagles grasp the nest with their talons and lift it off the ground. Before gaining momentum, Darvell looks back and calls out, "Goodbye! Good luck!"

Mikita watches the birds fly away until they are out of sight. She sighs and walks up the stairs to the back deck. Before reaching the top, her father's presence startles her. He is sitting on his mat cross-legged while meditating, as usual. Her mat is still sitting next to him. She pauses for a moment, regains her calm and confident center, then slowly removes her backpack, and sets it at the top of the stairs. She reaches her mat by walking with soft steps across the deck. Once she sits and gets comfortable, she closes her eyes and brief memories from her journey run through her mind. Devoid of any thoughts, she deeply feels the concepts she learned along the way and how they came together. By completing this practice, the concepts become more of who she is inside, they strengthen her intuition, and they will never leave her.

She opens her eyes and sees the sun lowering close enough to the horizon that the colors of sunset will appear soon. In heeding her father's instructions, she looks at him and says, "I'm home."

He opens his eyes and turns in her direction. "Why, Mikita, you have returned. How was your exploratory?"

She nods her head multiple times. "It was good. It was very adventurous."

"Did you find it enlightening?"

"Yes, I guess I didn't think about it that way but yes, it was very enlightening," A brief silence passes as Mikita looks around the yard then she suddenly exclaims, "Hey!"

"Hey, what?" asks her father.

"Where did my backpack go? I set it at the top of the stairs."

Her father turns to look at the woods. "Oh, I don't know. Perhaps your mother came and picked-it up already. You know, she is very efficient."

Mikita examines the side of his face, and a hint of a smile curves up the corner of his mouth. It reminds her of the joyous laughter of the new friends she met during her travels. She smiles too and simply says, "Perhaps."

The bird's evening songs escalate as Mikita says, "I'm ready. Let's plan the next season of services for the community."

"Are you sure that is in your heart?" asks Kitchwan.

"Positive. My heart is full now."

"Excellent. But for today, you should rest."

"Since everything is over, I'm getting tired."

Everything becomes bathed in the quiet colors of the sunset, and Mikita brings her hand near her mouth and yawns. She leans to the side and places her head on her father's shoulder. He responds likewise and places his hand on her back as they sit in silence until the sun disappears below the horizon.

New Beginning

Mikita opens her eyes after a long night's sleep. She notices that it's already light outside. Although she rested after her exploratory, she still has needed extra sleep. Since then, they scheduled the next season of Spiritual Practices Service and she surprised herself by spontaneously jotting down notes about her experiences. A memory here, a new thought there, and sometimes, a better way to express a concept. Before she knew it, she accumulated a pile of papers and handwritten pages. As she gets out of bed, she thinks about getting organized and figuring out her own way of creating formal writing.

After getting ready and eating some breakfast, she reaches the meditation room where her father is already moving forward with his day. "Good morning," she says.

"Good morning, Mikita. Feeling well rested?"

"Yes, I'm good. I've started some notes and would like to write soon. The passage we read before my journey was enlightening, but I was also wondering if there are writings about how all things change and evolve together in a way that makes each thing interconnected yet have uniqueness?"

"Those are interesting points of views. There is some, but I don't think there is much focus on how all things change combined with the coexistence of common interconnection and uniqueness."

"I see. I wonder if those things create the beauty and balance that makes up the rhythm of nature, of the world around us. I think that is part of the message I would like to focus on."

"Very good. I will pull a few books and passages for later this week. But for today, were you planning ongoing into town?"

"No, not really. Is there something you or mother need?"

"Well, no, but you could go to Yash's. He called this morning, and your outfit is ready."

"Outfit? I didn't order anything," says Mikita.

Kitchwan draws a hint of a smile. "Your first set of traditional practice linens is ready. You have earned it and are ready to become established." He sits at the desk and puts on his wire-rimmed glasses, the same as every other day.

"Really? This is taking me by surprise. I guess I knew it would happen someday but wasn't thinking about it much."

He looks over his glasses. "You can wait and go later this week."

"No, no." Stuck in the spot that she is standing, Mikita stares at her father. It's a great honor to be given traditional practice linens. He had to have something more to say.

Kitchwan finally confirms the traditions. "You can wear them to service this weekend. We will have a brief ceremony during service, then a celebration afterward."

Her heart fills with warmness. She swiftly walks around the desk and gives her father a sideways hug as he sits in the chair. "Okay, okay. I will go right now," she says before leaving the meditation room.

Caresse spies Mikita headed for the front door and says, "Don't forget to grab a jacket!"

"Why? Is it supposed to rain today? Not, the rain!"

"No, it's chilly outside. It's fall, you know."

"Alright, Mama." Mikita opens the closet door and grabs a light jacket. She probably won't need one, but it is a simple thing to do that will make her mother happy. After rushing out the door, she hurries down the sidewalk until she reaches the turn onto Main Street. There she slows her pace to enjoy all the greetings that she will share with everyone as they pass by one another.

Shortly after turning the corner, she sees Mr. Reedy. He reminds her of her adventures, and she smiles.

"Hello Mikita, you look well today."

"Thank you." Before passing him by, she stops and asks, "How are you today?"

"Me? I'm good. Just picked-up a few things to finish a landscaping project at home."

"How nice! I'm sure it will be beautiful when you're done."

"Thank you." He slightly bows his head, "Good day."

"You also, have a good day," she says before continuing into town.

Once she reaches Ellen's gallery, she pauses and taps on the window. Ellen turns and gives her a smile and a wave. Thomas is standing next to her, and they are with another gentleman. They are looking at new artwork hung on the sidewall and more pieces sit on the floor. "*It must be an artist who is displaying their work in the shop.*"

Mikita waves back at Ellen and notices there are also patrons in the front of the store admiring her work.

A few steps away from the gallery, she spies her friend Alan coming in her direction. Since he is taller than her, Mikita lifts her chin before making eye contact. He responds by slowing as they approach one another on the sidewalk.

"I heard you had the crowd going at the high school baseball game yesterday," she says.

"It was fun. In the eighth inning I made it to third base on a line-drive, then Rohan batted me in for the winning run."

"You really have found your unique talent," she replies with a nod and smile.

He bounces his head a few times. "Yah, thanks. It looks like I'll be going to the university on a baseball scholarship this fall."

"Really? I would like to hear more about how you got into baseball and your plans. Are you attending services this weekend?"

He shrugs. "Yah, I'll be there. I'm not sure what I can tell you, but I'll see you then."

"You probably know more than you realize. I look forward to talking to you." Mikita pulls herself away from where they are conversing, and they head off in different directions.

She arrives at Yash's and enters the shop. Yash is at the counter finishing business with another customer. Mikita passes the time by looking at samples the shop has on display. There is almost any fabric in any color which anyone can desire, but what makes his outfits impressive is the detail work and the embroidery. She runs her fingers along a swath of soft flannel until Yash's voice radiates in her direction.

"Hello, Mikita. We have something special for you today."

"I heard," she says with a bright smile and a blush rising up her cheeks.

He turns his head toward the backroom while keeping his eyes on Mikita. "Anya, she's here! Would you bring out the linens?"

Anya's voice travels from the next room. "Yes, of course. Just a moment."

Yash leads Mikita over to the display counter. "Let's open it over here, so you can get a good look at them before you try them on."

She follows him to the counter. Anya appears from the back room with a large gift box. While setting it down, she says, "This is very special for many reasons. We are so glad for you and Yash spent days working on it."

Yash flashes Anya a stare before encouraging Mikita. "Go ahead, open it."

Mikita feels curiosity welling inside. Sure, this was a special occasion, but traditional linens are just that, traditional linens. They aren't fancy or anything. She looks at them both with a keen eye, raising one eyebrow as her mother does sometimes. After turning her attention to the box, she pulls one of the deep blue ribbons to untie the bow and slides the ribbon off the box. Just as she is about to open the lid, Yash and Anya take a step closer to each other and Anya leans on Yash's shoulder.

"What? What are you two gushing about?" Mikita asks.

"Just open it," replies Yash.

She lifts the box and in it lay the tunic neatly folded on top. It's made of soft light green fabric, and unlike any traditional linen she had ever seen, along the neckline and cuffs, there are meticulously embroidered purple flowers mixed with winding deep green stems and leaves. "Oh, it's beautiful," she gasps before putting her hand over her mouth. The flowers were the same as the one her father gave her when she was little, and they remind her of the flower bud she had dreamt about in her sleep. She pulls the tunic out of the box and holds it up. "I see now," she says.

"There is also embroidery on the cuffs of the pants," says Yash.

She pulls the pants out of the box, and they are just as detailed as the tunic.

"Try it on! We want to be sure it's perfect for this weekend," says Anya.

Mikita says nothing more and takes the outfit to the dressing room. While changing, she also notices Yash tailored them similar to the way he usually creates her other outfits. She feels her eyes burn and tears welling in their base, so she takes a moment to ground herself and embrace her emotions before walking out of the dressing room.

Once she exits, Yash sees her and says, "Oh yes, that's lovely. Come stand in the fitting area so I can make my inspection."

Anya stands alongside and clasps her hands together. "We think your mother also had something to do with all this. She was the one who made the order."

"That wouldn't surprise me." Mikita looks at Anya and they share a giggle.

"You seem so radiant and happy," says Anya.

Yash finishes his inspection and takes a step back. "It looks wonderful to me."

Anya leans forward. "There you are!"

Mikita looks at them both and says, "Yes, here I am."

GARETH

Hanging On

Gareth sits at his desk where he can see the Kravin Architecture logo on the wall just across from his office. Henry Kravin, his boss, runs the firm. The team just finished their largest projects and things have come to the pace of water dripping out of an old faucet. Happy to be in his own world, he fiddles with a model of the sprawling twelve-story building that he hopes to build someday. It has one large square formation in the center and growing out of that are smaller formations on each side. The roof of each of the smaller scrapers creates large terraces with green spaces.

His colleague, Lem, stops outside his door and asks, "Are you ready?"

"Ready for what?" Gareth sits straight up. "Did I miss something?"

"Oh man, you have to read your email more often. Henry sent out a message this morning. We have a meeting with Nova Investment in a few minutes."

"Really? With no time to prepare?"

Lem leans his thin body against the doorframe. "Don't worry. It's a huge project they are presenting to multiple firms. We just have to listen."

"Is that supposed to make me feel better?" Gareth grabs his tie off the back of the chair. "Do you think this tie matches what I'm wearing? It's the only one I have in the office."

"It's fine. With your dress shirt buttoned all the way to the top, you're practically ready to roll," Lem says.

Gareth gives Lem a piercing look as he tightens the tie. He runs his hands through his hair, so it makes tussled waves before sliding on his suit jacket.

Their colleague, Asmee, appears behind Lem in the hallway. She stops and gives them her biggest smile. Lem leans in her direction while continuing to prop himself on the doorframe.

Asmee's mascara enhanced eyelashes raise closer to her eyebrows as she says, "Good Morning. Are you guys ready? The owner of Nova will be here for the presentation. I guess it's for a large office and apartment building here in the city."

Gareth and Lem's eyes lock for a second. Neither of them takes the bait and asks what else she knows about the project.

"Morning Asmee. I'm sure everyone is looking forward to the meeting," Lem replies.

"It's very exciting," Asmee says over her should as she walks down the hallway. Her high heel shoes click on the tile with each step until the sound fades away.

Gareth shakes his head and returns to straightening the collar of his suit jacket. Now satisfied with his appearance, he walks with Lem towards the conference room.

They turn the corner and Gareth sees Henry Kravin sitting at the end of the table and three people sitting on the other side, closer to the presentation screen. Asmee is sitting next to Henry with her back to the door. Booklets are neatly laid out on the wooden conference table in front of two chairs next to Asmee. He reaches for his pen in his breast pocket and realizes it's not there. His mind thinks uncontrollably. "*I can't go into this meeting without a pen. That would be terrible. What if I need to write something down? Worse yet, what if it's suggested I write a detail down? Besides, I need something to hold in my hands…*"

"I need to get my pen," says Gareth.

"Here I have an extra." Lem pulls a pen out of his jacket pocket.

"No, no. I need my pen. The one that Caitlin gave me."

"Oh man, all right. If things settle down before you return, I'll tell them you're on your way."

Gareth rushes back to his office. His breath quickens and itchy heat spreads throughout his neck and shoulders. He searches the table around the model of the building and the top of the desk. His heartbeat increases as he pushes papers aside to reveal the etched silver pen. He picks up the pen and as the cold metal warms in his hand, he begins to return to normal.

The Challenge

Gareth takes the seat next to Lem and pulls the chair closer to the conference table. Outside the window is a view of the city and the mountains in the distance. He pulls in a deep breath through his nose and exhales.

Henry clears his throat. "All right everyone, let's get started." He lets silence take over the room. "Today we have some guests from Nova Investment to tell us about an opportunity for our architecture firm." Henry nods towards each of them as he says, "We have Nirvaan, the owner, Juhi, their Business Administrator and Robert, another associate within the company."

Nirvaan addresses the table next. "We're glad to be here today. Your firm has an excellent reputation, and your team has impressive credentials. We look forward to seeing your proposals for our project."

Henry shifts in his chair. "Thank you. We're also glad you're here today. Everyone knows me, I'm Henry Kravin." He gestures to the other side of the table. "This is Asmee. She has been with Kravin Architecture since the very beginning, and has successfully completed many projects, including the Colleridge Skyscraper in our neighbor city of Summit."

Asmee grows an enormous smile and nods. "Nice to meet you."

Henry shifts his gesture. "This is Lem. He is an excellent leader and specializes in blending the outside architectural design elements into the interior designs of buildings."

"Hello. Happy to be here," replies Lem.

"And to finish the introductions, this is Gareth. He is the newest member of our team. He comes with the highest academic credentials and just finished building a pair of grocery stores with Nature's Basket."

Gareth runs his thumb along the pen, then makes eye contact with the group from the investment company. "Good to meet everyone."

"This is our team, and whomever creates the concept accepted by Nova will be the lead. This team has worked together superbly and has been very successful." Henry looks at Nirvaan.

Gareth watches as Nirvaan turns to meet eyes with Henry. Nirvaan's face remains completely expressionless. Gareth can't even note the slightest tick of a muscle.

After the failed exchange of confidence, Henry says, "Great. With that, I will turn the meeting over to Nirvaan."

Nirvaan nods. "Robert is an associate with our team, and he will be making the initial presentation today."

"Thanks, Nirvaan," Robert stands from his chair and flicks on the large screen with a remote.

Robert positions himself next to the screen. The illustrations on the first slide include a couple of graphs. "For the last two years, Nova has conducted extensive research about the needs of Rolling Hill City. Historically, the city has been a location where people pass through while traveling the Great Mountains that surround the city's west and northwest sides. Despite Rolling Hill has become the largest city in the area, there is a lack of living spaces. At the same time, the number of employment positions has increased at a rapid rate." Robert points to a graph with an upward trajectory.

He advances to the next slide that has a map of the surrounding area. "In addition, the average commute into the city is over sixteen minutes. In fact, they range between twelve minutes from the town of Jasmuth, which is northeast of the city, to almost twenty-five minutes from Krane located southeast of the city."

After walking over to the other side of the screen, Robert advances to the next slide with a list of bullet points. "In our polling, we found that the people who would consider moving to Rolling Hill want convenience. They want high-end apartments and a lifestyle that is free from things such as mortgages and maintaining a property." He pauses for a moment. "We also found that business owners want spaces that are flexible and can accommodate growing operations. Then, we found that both groups would choose a location that is environmentally conscious over others, even if the rent is slightly more expensive."

The following slide, he boldly titled, "The Project." And it only has a few key points. "We have two Rolling Hill locations in mind, one near the center of downtown and another on the northwest edge of the city, but we will build in only one location. Ultimately Nova is looking to create a modern building that is environmentally friendly, contains luxury apartments and flexible office spaces." He scans everyone at the conference table and raises a closed hand. "A building that will change the skyline of the city. One that is ultra-modern and creates a community. A place that welcomes everyone who takes part in the city." At the close, Robert lowers his hand.

Everyone at the table gives Robert a short applause then turns to Nirvaan. Gareth gets a wave of lightheadedness at the thought of creating an iconic building in the city. His grip tightens on his pen, and he looks down so he can draw in another deep breath.

As expected, Nirvaan addresses the table. "The key concepts are a building that will change the skyline and is ultra-modern. Don't come to me with a building that looks the same as everything else. We want something that stands-out while complementing the rest of the city and the surrounding mountains."

Gareth watches Nirvaan, still searching for a change in his facial expression.

Nirvaan continues his instructions. "In front of you is a packet. In it are all the details including site locations, size of the properties and proposed budget. It also includes more about the demographics of the expected consumers."

Finally, Nirvaan raises his eyebrows while widening his eyes. Gareth feels his gaze and words penetrate his brain as he says, "Review it carefully. We expect this building to appeal to a wide variety of people, including businesspeople in the area and those who want to live in the city to be close to the mountains or where they work. We will schedule a return visit in approximately a month to hear presentations of your concepts. For any of them to succeed, they must address all the details outlined."

Gareth looks over to Juhi, Nova's Business Administrator who is sitting next to Nirvaan. She looks back and pushes her glasses up her nose while giving him a nonchalant nod. As Gareth's sight glides over to Robert, he takes on his predecessor's behavior and sits without additional expression. Then he turns his attention to Henry at the other end of the table. Out of the corner of his eye, he sees Asmee pick up some pages of the booklet and let them fall back onto the table, revealing her disinterest in the contents.

"Well, thank you and we look forward to presenting the vision for your next building." Henry stands-up and everyone follows suit. All of them shake hands and make small talk until one by one they exit the conference room.

Gareth returns to his office with long strides and plops down in his desk chair. He holds the pen and spins the chair until he's looking at the model. "*Lem sure called that one. No reason to prepare for that meeting. It's an interesting turn of events, but my building isn't quite ultra-modern and it's way too big for a downtown location. It's going to take a slam dunk to get this account. I'm not sure I'm up for all of it*," he thinks. Still moving forward, he turns his chair back towards the desk and pours over the booklet provided by Nova.

The rest of the afternoon remains quiet and Gareth packs-up his leather over the should bag. He digs his keys out of one of the front pockets and heads to his car. While driving out of the city, he inspects the buildings and skyline, thinking about how an ultra-modern building might look and lets all the information from Nova gel in his mind. Before he knows it, he's on the highway headed for home and then the "Welcome to Krane" sign appears.

Comfort and familiarity overcome him as he pulls into the drive of his house. It's a traditional design with white siding and a tree in the front yard. It's not fancy, but that was the point when he and Catlin picked it out. He remembers when they looked at it for the first time. Her face brightened, and she smiled before they even walked inside. As soon as they passed the threshold of the front door, she turned to him and nodded. "This is home," she said.

A heaviness settles into Gareth's chest, so he lets the brief memory pass as he puts the car in park. He grabs his bag and walks up the sidewalk followed by the small steps to the house. As soon as he opens the door, he hears Alysia's cheerful voice.

"Daddy's home!" Alysia comes running around the corner.

Gareth's heart completely lightens, and he bends down, ready to swoop her into a big hug while he says, "Hello!" He ends the embrace and puts his bag on the floor. "What did you do today?"

"Oh, we made collages out of tissue paper. It was fun! Mine is in the kitchen." Alysia runs away to retrieve her artwork.

"Hello, Emma?" calls Gareth.

Emma appears from the kitchen and Alysia does a swerve to get past her. "Hey Gareth, how was work?"

"It was interesting. We had an unexpected meeting."

"Oh, that sounds intriguing."

Alysia bolts across the room with a large piece of paper decorated with bright tissue paper pieces. "See, it's a big rainbow with all the colors."

Gareth sits on the couch and Alysia jumps up to sit next to him. He holds one end of the paper so they can look at it together. Alysia starts again using her finger as a pointer. "Here is the big rainbow. Then here's the sun and the rain clouds in the sky."

Gareth gives her a squeeze. "Wow! That's great. I really like your choice of colors."

"Yah, Aunt Emma said the same thing."

Gareth looks at Emma and they exchange a smile. Alysia jumps off the couch. With the rainbow collage flapping behind her and her brown curly hair bouncing, she runs across the living room.

"Where are you going?" asks Gareth.

"I'm going to my bedroom to show my collage to all my animals so we can all sit under the rainbow." And she disappears down the hallway.

"Okay, have fun," says Gareth. He leans back in the couch.

"So, what happened at work today?" Emma probes him further.

"There are investors who want to build a large office space and apartment building in the city."

"Really? Are you going to go for it?"

"Well, sure but…"

"But what? You have the talent and the vision. You'd be fantastic," says Emma.

"Thanks, I'm just not sure if I'm up for it right now."

Gareth senses a shift of energy in the room. He watches Emma as she walks over and sits on the couch next to him. She looks at the ground and nods a couple of times before looking him in the eye. "You know, staying in the same place won't bring her back."

Gareth turns away from Emma. "I know," he mumbles. "I just miss her."

"Caitlin was my baby sister and I miss her too, but she would want you to be successful. What happened, that she got sick, and no one could help her wasn't your fault."

"I hear you, thanks. I'll put my heart into it a little more."

"I wish you would allow yourself to do that, you know, give yourself permission, to be happy. It's been a long time now."

Gareth stands and takes a few steps to the kitchen. "I have to check what we have for dinner."

Emma lets out a radiating sigh. "Sure, of course. I have to get home myself." She grabs her coat from the other side of the couch, slips it on and picks up her purse. She faces the hallway before saying, "Alysia, I'm going to get going now. I'll see you tomorrow after school."

Alysia's voice carries from the hallway. "Wait, Aunt Emma. Let me give you a goodbye hug." Flying around the corner, Alysia continues to where Emma is standing and gives her a hug.

Emma responds and leans over enough so she can pat Emma's back. "My, I wish I had as much energy as you. See you tomorrow."

While holding on to the opened door, Alysia calls out one last farewell, "Bye-bye, Aunt Emma!" She closes the door and runs back to her room.

Gareth makes dinner and gets the table set. Just as he is finishing, he thinks, "*Alysia has such an imagination.*

She can play with her stuffed animals for hours without a care in the world."

Gareth calls out, "Alysia, it's time for dinner. It's your favorite, angel hair pasta."

He smiles when he faintly hears her say, "All right." Then, moving at her normal hyper-speed, she appears at the table.

Gareth fills his plate with the pasta coated with olive oil and tossed with vegetables before serving Alysia. The aroma at the table is intoxicating.

Content with her meal, Alysia fills her first fork full and lifts the pasta to her mouth. As they both enjoy their dinner, the silence stretches into a few minutes.

After a bite, Alysia pauses and says, "I heard you and Aunt Emma talking about Mom."

Gareth puts his fork down and looks at her. "Oh, yah? What did you hear?"

"I was going to the living room to see if you wanted to make a collage with me, and you said that you miss her. Then Aunt Emma said she missed her too, but Mom would want you to be happy."

"I see. How did that make you feel?"

Alysia tilts her head, then twirls a few strands of the fine pasta around her fork. "I miss mom sometimes too, but I don't feel so sad anymore and I don't want you to be sad."

"Oh, honey. I don't feel sad. That's not exactly what Aunt Emma meant. It was more about work and stuff. I'm happy and I'm really happy when I get to spend time with you, and we do fun things. It would be cool to make a collage with you, maybe this weekend."

"Yah! I would like to make a collage again." Alysia plays with her pasta a little more. "I'm glad you're not sad."

"Me too." Gareth eats another fork full of pasta. He follows it with a drink of water. "You know, Mom loved you very much. She loved both of us and in a way she still does." He puts down his fork and tickles her chest until she crunches her shoulders together and bursts with laughter. "Her love is still right there."

"Stop! Stop! I get it." Alysia squirms and Gareth settles back in his chair.

"Now, let me finish my dinner," she says.

"You are amazing," replies Gareth.

Start Somewhere

After arriving at the office, Gareth finishes reviewing the booklet. He looks at the notepad, and his notes are almost as long as the booklet. Turning once again to his model, he feels paralyzed and does nothing but stare at the balsa wood pieces with a blank mind.

"Oh man, that's not going to make it look any different," says Lem.

Gareth raises his head to shoot Lem a piercing stare, but Lem's untucked shirt and lose-fitting khaki pants match his sense of humor, so he laughs instead. "I know, there's just something that's not right, and it takes up too much space for the downtown site."

"So? Isn't there a site on the edge of the city to consider? I'm sure that one is bigger."

"Well, sure, but how is anything besides a skyscraper supposed to change the skyline of the city?"

Lem stares at Gareth. "Really? You have to ask? What is the first building you think of in Jasmuth?"

"Jasmuth? The Walsh and Weaks Art Museum, of course. It takes on the more traditional neo-classic style of the City Hall mixed with an art déco style that accents the sky dome."

"What else is great about the Art Museum in Jasmuth?" asks Lem.

"It's blend of architecture with the sky dome complements the smooth hills that surround Jasmuth."

"Right. And what about in Summit?"

"In Summit it's the Goethe Orchestra Hall. Now, that's iconic."

"Why?" Lem pushes.

"We all know why; its post-modern curves replicate the rolling swells on Lake Summit where it's located."

"And are either of them the tallest structure in the skyline?"

"Got it. I see your point." Gareth opens the booklet from Nova again and scans the page with the map of sites. "Yes, the northwest site runs up to the park and over half the building would have an unobstructed view of the mountains."

Lem walks behind Gareth and looks over his should at the map. "Seems like a good place to live and work to me."

Gareth spies Asmee outside his door and motions his chin in her general direction. Lem lifts his head and extends a greeting, "Hello, Asmee. What are you up to today?"

"You know, the same as always. Well, except for working-up a concept to pitch to Nirvaan. I get a good feeling about this one." She puts her hand lightly on her chest. "I mean, I've already built one skyscraper."

"Does that mean you are going to focus on the downtown site?" Gareth asks in a casual tone.

"Of course. What else is there? Besides, why are you guys worrying about the booklet? Most clients don't know what they really want until you tell them."

Lem straightens from leaning over Gareth's shoulder. "I suppose you could be right."

"I know I'm right," Asmee replies. She pulls her dark blue polyester suit jacket down before continuing on her way.

Gareth and Lem stare at the empty doorway for a few beats. Gareth shakes his head, and says, "I really get what you are saying now." He clears his throat. "Even if the northwest site is the way to go, there is still something off about the concept I have started."

Lem looks at the model and puts his hand over his mouth. He slides it to see another angle and leans to view it from the side. "Well, the green spaces on each of the terraces fit with the client's requests of it appealing to an environmentally conscious renter."

Gareth nods and stands next to Lem. "Yes, that's exactly what I was thinking, but they're too big. If they would be common areas, that reduces privacy or if they are private, that would limit them to the high-income renters."

"For sure," says Lem. "Architecture is my passion and I've been in the business a long time, but I don't want to build buildings from scratch. As most everyone knows, I appreciate that in an iconic building, the outside architecture blends with the inside architecture and that's important."

"Yes, but what are you getting at?"

"It's simple really, if you're stuck on how the outside should exactly look, think about how the inside should work. Then you can go back to the outside concept. Let one create the other."

"Brilliant. That's an excellent point, especially for this client."

"Well, thanks." Lem nods. "Nova certainly has distinct ideas about the details of how the building should function." He leaves the office but pauses at the door. "You could try letting it go for a bit, get out of the office. You have time, just let things take their course and everything will be fine."

Left alone in his office again, Gareth picks up his pen and runs his fingers along the sides so he can feel the etchings. "*Lem is right again in so many ways. Get out of the office. Grab your coat it's a beautiful day*," he thinks.

Once outside, Gareth wanders the city surrounding where the architectural firm is located. It's been a while since he enjoyed the unique buildings and people watching. His coat shields him from the brisk spring day and allows the bright sunshine to warm his insides. He sees people moving about and restaurants bustling with lunchtime patrons. He imagines many of them only have an hour to enjoy lunch outside of the office. Then, looking at the tops of the buildings and skyscrapers, he inspects how many of them have spires of all different types and shapes. Some are more traditional, built of gray stone that swiftly comes to a single point and some are more modern, made of reflective sliver and terraced so they gradually rise together.

A passerby brushes his arm, and she slows to say, "Excuse me."

Gareth's focus returns to what is happening on the ground, and replies, "No problem."

The passerby is out of ear shot, but Gareth notices she is part of a distinct stream of people headed in the same direction. He joins the stream to investigate where everyone is going. They flow off the main sidewalk onto a worn path that goes up a small hill. Once he reaches the top of the hill, he sees a large open-air market filling an old parking lot. "*I had no idea this was here. I wonder how long I've been oblivious to all this activity. Amazing.*"

The variety of stands in the market is remarkable. Artwork of every kind, handcrafted jewelry, refurbished furniture, more and more. One end of the lot has stands full of fresh foods, including fresh produce. He notices the fresh produce stands have semi-permanent wooden structures. In between two large sellers he spies a small booth where a young woman with her hair in a long braid is selling local honey and a variety of cheeses. The sunlight makes the golden-brown honey look extra appealing. Many people are enjoying the market, so he bumbles across the people-traffic to approach the stand. "Hello. How are you today?"

She shifts her attention to him and replies, "Hello. I'm good. What can I help you with?"

"I'll take one of your medium jars of honey."

"Excellent choice. We rarely have honey this early in the year, but somehow, we ended-up with a little extra inventory from the fall. Our mistake is your gain."

"Lucky for me. I grew-up on a farm and we had honeybees. It was pretty cool, and I miss raw honey." He watches the woman package the honey jar into a paper bag. "How long has this market been going on?"

She hands him the bag and squints as the sunlight hits her eyes. "I'm not sure, two, maybe three years. Everyone's excited, we just opened for the season."

Gareth hands her the money to pay for the honey. "I'm surprised how busy it is since it's kind of brisk out today."

"Well, you know us Rolling Hill and Great Mountain folks, always ready to get out and enjoy a sunny day," she says, followed by a small laugh.

On his way back to the office, Gareth takes in the sites again, including the architecture of the buildings and activity of the people. He's filled with a sense of wonder about how walking in the other direction gives everything an entirely new perspective. Even the building that he works at everyday takes on a fresh look as enters the front doors, since normally he would come through the parking garage. It's a bit of a letdown when he is immediately met by a dull elevator bay. "*Is there even a lobby in this place?*" he wonders.

He passes the elevators to examine the lobby. The floor is covered with large tan tiles, the space is two stories high, and the ceiling is white with a few minimalist light fixtures. There is some furniture and a few plants arranged in front of a security guard station that probably also serves as an information desk. There is no one occupying the furniture despite it's still the lunch hours. The space is left empty and cold.

Gareth shakes his head as he hits the elevator button. Then it comes to him, he knows how to make improvements in his building. The thoughts and images skip through his mind, demanding they be poured out in expression. He hits the tenth-floor button on the elevator pad an extra time. Finally getting to his office, he sets the bag with honey on the desk and flings off his jacket. He turns to the model and walks around it a few times. Then he encourages himself. "*I can do this. The model won't be for the presentation but just start here. You can transfer it over to modeling software when you're ready.*"

Gareth opens the box sitting next to balsa wood model and takes out the smallest hobby knife with a carving blade. He holds the knife like a surgeon and cuts out open spaces around the ground floor of his model. Spaces that can be open or closed to the outside through well-designed glass roll-up doors. On nice days, this would give it the feel of the open-air market. These are perfect places for local businesses like retail shops and restaurants. He finishes this around the building except for the shortest structures.

On the shortest structures, he cuts out large entrances that lead to an open atrium. He puts the knife back in the kit and grabs a thick drawing pencil. He takes one of the largest sheets of drawing paper and slides it under the model, leaving plenty of room to draw on the table. With a new vision of the largest scraper having a massive skylight as part of the roof and sunlight streaming all the way to the atrium, he sketches the inside. His hands move rapidly to keep-up with his imagination. He draws in entranceways to the business spaces so patrons can enter them from the outside or inside of the building. A smile grows on his face as images of people bustling about the atrium while going in and out of the establishments comes into his mind. He tosses the pencil down and looks at the clock. It had gotten late. He has to get home before he holds-up Emma. As always, he packs his bag but makes sure not to forget the honey sitting on his desk.

⁂

Gareth closes the front door to the house with a thump. He realizes he feels different somehow, that he is standing taller.

"Daddy's Home," Alysia says with excitement, and he can hear her coming down the hallway.

He smiles and waits for her to come into view. She runs towards him, and he leans over for their daily hug. He hugs her and swings her in a half circle.

"Whoa!" she exclaims, then laughs.

Gareth laughs too as he gently settles her on the ground. "Hello yourself! What's new?"

"Nothing, really. Aunt Emma let me build a fort in my bedroom. I want to go back and play. Will you come see it?"

"Sure, but in a little bit. I just got home."

"Oh, okay." Alysia turns and runs back to her bedroom.

Gareth puts his bag down and hangs his coat in the entryway closet. Just as he flops down on the couch, Emma comes in from the kitchen.

"Hey, welcome home. How are you today?" she asks.

"I'm good. I had a productive day. Still haven't created what could be an iconic building or anything, but it was progress."

"That sounds promising."

"Yah, but I just can't get the building itself nailed down. I think my creativity is stuck."

"Your creativity, huh." Emma sits on the chair across the living room. "Hey, I have an idea."

"You're going to build buildings now?" Gareth laughs.

"Oh, stop!" She playfully swings her hand in the air. "Why don't you come to Spiritual Practices Service with me on Sunday?"

"Spiritual Practices Service? Where?"

"In Tree Side Village. Some of the practices can be very good for stirring inner creativity, so I'm told."

"Okay. Why not? Caitlin and I used to take part in a group like that here in Krane."

Emma's voice takes on a higher pitch. "Really? I didn't know."

"Sure, we did it for many years. Then Alysia was born, and things got so hectic we stopped going and, well, never got back. Anyway, it would be good to shake-up the schedule, try something new." Gareth leans back into the cushions of the couch and swipes some fuzz off his pants.

"Super! Just come to my place at about 9:00."

"9:00 in the morning on a Sunday?" Gareth exaggerates with a roll of his eyes. "I didn't know that when I agreed."

"All right, why don't you meet me outside of the Community Center at 9:45? Services start at 10:00. Alysia can play at the Children's Recreation Center just down the hall. They keep a very watchful eye on all the kids. The same folks who run the daycare run the center. It's open for all the children of the participants."

"Okay, 9:45, at the Community Center is better." He laughs and tosses a pillow at Emma. "And so, you let Alysia build a fort?"

"Yes, she was disappointed because she doesn't have art class on Fridays, so I let her take sheets out of the closet and drag a couple of kitchen chairs into her room to make a fort. Last I checked, she had her animal friends in it for a visit."

"I'll never get her to take it down!" says Gareth.

"Your probably right. Well, like any good aunt, once the damage is done, it's time to go." Emma chuckles. She gets up, puts on her coat and grabs her purse. "Alysia, I'm going now. I'll see you later."

Alysia shouts from her bedroom. "Okay! I can't come out because I'm trapped in the fort. It's surrounded by a bunch of octopus monsters that walk on land."

"Oh well, look out!" Emma looks at Gareth and they both have a hearty laugh. "Have a good start to the weekend and I'll see you Sunday."

Gareth follows Emma to the door, then retrieves the honey from his work bag and stops in the kitchen to put it away before visiting Alysia's room. He stands in her doorway, eyeing the fort. Two overlapping sheets stream from being pinched in her top dresser drawer to being pinned with books on the seats of two chairs. There are additional sheets draped on the back of the chairs that reach to the floor. "Hello, are you still trapped by strange monsters?"

"No Daddy! We are in a boat on the high seas now. You'll have to swim for it," says Alysia in her most animated tone.

"Okay!" Then Gareth makes splashing noises and bends over, trying to find a way into the fort. "I can't get into the boat. Can you lend me a hand or something?"

Alysia lifts-up the sheet and pops her head out. "Here! Climb in here!"

Gareth crawls in the fort as best he can and sees all her stuffed animals lined-up on partially open dresser drawers. "Wow. Cool boat. It's almost time to report to the galley for dinner," he says.

"Can't I play a little longer? Please, please?"

He expected this response and hoped to use it to his advantage by laying the groundwork for more than dinner. "Oh, all right, you can play a little longer but then it's dinner, bath and bed sailor."

"Got it, sir. Dinner, bath and bed," she replies in a dramatic deep voice.

MIKITA

The Figures

Mikita allows herself to come out of meditation at a slow pace. She turns her focus away from the point just above the bridge of her nose and transitions to sensing a connection with the wood of the deck, then allows her eyes to open. The late evening colors blanket the budding trees and fine spring grass with an orange glow. Lately she enjoys an evening mediation to clear away the day and let the cool air invigorate her senses. She stands and collects the mats, then puts them away in the bin just inside the meditation room.

Mikita sees her father sitting at the desk with papers and an open book. "Hello, I'm surprised you're still here."

"Oh, I left and came back." He smiles and rubs the top of his head. "I wanted to write out a few thoughts and put them to rest for the night. I was just wrapping up."

She looks at the brass figures on the shelf in the meditation room. "Do you have time for a question?"

Kitchwan stands from the desk and collects the papers. "Of course." He puts the papers in a folder and neatly stacks the book on top. Once he's finished, he looks at Mikita.

"I've been having an intuition to change the brass figures in the morning and after meditating. I was wondering how picking and changing them normally works."

"Very good. We haven't talked about this yet." He walks over to the shelf with the figures to stand next to Mikita. "When they continue to call to you, you can switch them out." He walks over to a closet in the meditation room and opens the door. "They are kept in here."

Mikita peers into the closet. "I was wondering what is in here." One side of the closet has shelves with brass figures arranged in neat rows. "I didn't know there are so many."

"Yes. Over the years practitioners have added to the collection. I wasn't inspired to do that, but you might be. Basically, that's an individual choice." Kitchwan pulls the string hanging from the lightbulb fixture on the ceiling. A dim light fills the closet. "You can develop a way to manage them that works for you. I've made a ritual out of the practice."

"How do you know which ones to put out?" asks Mikita.

"You don't, really. There is no right or wrong answer, just use your intuition. Sometimes after they are out for a while, they make perfect sense." Kitchwan draws a closed-mouth smile while eyeing the figures. "Sometimes they change again and again for seemingly no reason."

"I see." Mikita steps further into the closet.

"Normally I start by focusing on the ones on the display shelf." Kitchwan heads back that direction. "Sometimes, I don't feel the need to change them all, so I start with the ones that are most obvious."

Mikita stands next to her father in front of the figures. "Let's start with these two. I feel it's time to put them back." She removes the skilled fish from under the sea and the beaver who lives both in and out of the pond, leaving the antelope that dances across the land and the bird who soars through the air on the shelf. Then she returns to the closet, and places those back next to similar type of figures.

Kitchwan remains standing a few steps away from the closet. "When one calls to you or jumps out to you, pick that one. Try not to think about it so much. If you don't know exactly what the figure is depicting, that's okay. You can research that later and learning about the figure might be its significance."

Mikita is overwhelmed by the number of choices. As her father mentioned, she's not familiar with all the subjects of the figures. Quickly, one jumps out at her. She removes it from the shelf. It must not have been displayed in a long time because it's covered with a thick coat of dust. She blows on it a little.

"There is a soft cloth sitting near the door. You can use that to clean it for display," says Kitchwan.

Mikita cleans off the figure and places the cloth back in place. She notices another figure and picks that one out. She continues the ritual and gets them both cleaned and polished. After that she walks out with the new figures. "Ok, these two for sure." She places them in the empty spots on the shelf but senses a pinprick in her chest. "Does the order mater?"

"It can, yes," her father replies.

Mikita turns back to focus on the figures. She picks up the antelope that dances across the land. "The antelope stays, but I should move it down second from last." Now she is holding the bird that soars through the air. She looks at the bird, it's good but not quite right. "I will change this one, too."

"Very good." Kitchwan allows Mikita to proceed on her own.

Mikita puts the soaring bird in the closet and spies another bird figure that looks just right. She grabs that figure but becomes confused because another bird jumps out to her. She picks that one up also and walks out to look at her father. "What if two figures jump out at you?"

"Are they similar?" he asks.

She looks at the details of each. "Yes, very."

"Either will probably be fine. You can pick the one you saw first or the one that calls out to you more."

"Okay, they both seem equal so I will pick the one I saw first." Mikita cleans the figure and returns to the display shelf. She rearranges the figures some more and then stands back to examine her work. Nodding, she says, "I think that's it."

"Let's see what you have." Kitchwan steps closer. "The bee who fills the honeycomb with nectar, the bird who courts in the flowers, the antelope that dances across the land, and…" He pauses and rubs his head.

"And?" asks Mikita. "I'm not sure exactly what it's depicting, but it was the first one I picked out."

"And nothing, it's just interesting. You have an interesting mix of symbols. The last one is the crafty termite who is a master builder. I think they live in the far reaches of grasslands where they meet with the savannas."

"Termites? They are creepy looking."

"I guess but pay that no mind. They are all part of the beauty and balance of nature." Kitchwan turns and walks with quick steps towards the bookshelves. He runs his fingers along the spines and picks one to take back to the desk. After settling in the chair, he puts on his glasses and opens the book.

While watching him, Mikita's stomach feels like it's being infused with static electricity. Her brow furrows as she gets comfortable on the other chair. "What are you reading?"

Kitchwan spends an elongated moment examining some passages in the book and flipping to a map in the appendix. "Yes, see here. They live in the farthest reaches of the grasslands. They build huge hills or mounds and thrive there as a community. No one is sure how they fit into the interconnection of all things."

"It's interesting, that's for sure," says Mikita.

"Well, I will mark the page so you can read more if you remain interested." Kitchwan closes the book and removes his glasses so he can rub his eyes.

"Thanks, I will look at it later. It seems like a good time to call it a day."

"Yes, I suppose you are right. I already ended my day once." Kitchwan chuckles. "Tomorrow we can review the plan for services this weekend to make sure you are comfortable. This will be the first time I won't be attending."

"I know. I can't believe the winter season is over already. It went by so quickly."

"Well, you are ready, and I will be here to advise you all that you need." Kitchwan stands waiting for Mikita to do the same.

“Thank you, father. It’s both exciting and a little scary.”

“Aren’t they both one and the same emotion?” Kitchwan says, and they both laugh while walking out of the meditation room.

Gareth

Past and Present

Gareth opens his eyes and from what he can see through the edges of the window blinds, it's a cloudy day. He stretches and smiles because he slept well. No tossing and turning, just deep restful sleep. Pulling-up the warm covers, he snuggles in and allows himself to doze off again until he hears the TV on in the living room. He pulls the covers back. "*I never imagined being a single parent. It's completely overwhelming.*"

This sets off a reflection in his mind and memories come like fresh popcorn popping in a hot oiled skillet. Emma was always there. She was there when Caitlin was sick and when Caitlin died. She was there for him and Alysia through the funeral. Then when he went back to work, she started picking Alysia up after school and bringing her home. At home she cared for Alysia. Until he got home, Emma got her snacks, watched over her, entertained her, and sometimes even disciplined her. Emma did all of this without question, without having to be asked. She was always there. "*Alysia loves Emma and I rely on her. I haven't thanked her for so long and need to thank her more often.*"

Gareth gets out of bed and puts his pajama top on over his lean but athletically muscular torso, then pulls on his robe. His feet stumble down the hallway as he ties the robe and blinks his eyes. Alysia is sitting on the living room floor in front of the television. He says, "Good morning. I'll get breakfast started in a minute."

"Hi Daddy, look at this."

Gareth sits down on the chair in the living room. "What are you watching?"

"Public television, they are doing a series of shows about birds in the forest and the Great Mountains. I think it's cool."

He watches a small black bird with outstretched oval shaped wings rhythmically jump from side to side while it makes clicking sounds. The bottom of each wing is accented with a teal stripe that stands out. Not awake enough to process much, he asks, "What is that bird doing?"

"What does it look like he's doing? He's dancing."

Gareth can't help but make sense of the scene. "Is that a real bird? Why in the world is he doing that?"

"Of course, it's a real bird. I told you; this is a show on public television. He's dancing to attract a bird-mate."

Gareth stands from the chair. "Golly! Don't you want to be watching cartoons or something, I don't know, more fun?"

"Not really," Alysia says while keeping her eyes focused on the screen.

"You are amazing," he mumbles as he heads to the kitchen to put breakfast together. He pulls the bread out of the cupboard along with the peanut butter and honey. Then he gathers-up two plates and sets them on the table next to fresh bananas perched in plain sight.

Alysia hears him rummaging in the kitchen and asks, "What are you doing?"

"I'm making peanut butter banana sandwiches with honey. Why don't you come and get the toast started?"

As Gareth expected, this intrigues Alysia, so she trots into the kitchen and slides her step stool to a prime location. After stepping up, she opens the bread and takes two slices from the middle of the loaf to stuff into the toaster. Once she pushes down the plunger, she returns to stand by the table. "What's with the honey? We don't normally have honey."

"I know, but that's how I had peanut butter banana sandwiches when I was your age. Give it a chance, it's good." Gareth notices Alysia's pout. "If you don't like it with the honey, we'll make one without. Deal?"

"Okay, deal."

"Now, you can slice the bananas." He puts a small cutting board on the table and hands her a butter knife. Then he demonstrates while saying, "See, make the slices about this big so they are the right size for the sandwich."

Alysia watches him and goes to work. "Like this?" she asks.

"Yes, that's perfect." He places another peeled banana on the cutting board. "One more to go, take your time."

The toast pops out of the toaster and Gareth places them on a plate. He carefully smears one slice with peanut butter. Then he takes the honey jar and sets it on the table next to Alysia. He tosses two more pieces of bread into the toaster. "Okay, lay the banana slices on top of the peanut butter. Don't worry about how many you use, lay them so they cover the bread."

Alysia looks at him. "Kind of like a collage?"

He smiles. "Yes, just like a collage."

Once she finishes, he says, "Okay, I will put the honey on top." He dips a small spoon in the jar and hoovers it over the sandwich, so the honey slowly drizzles off the spoon. Once the stream hits the sandwich, he moves spoon up and down the banana rows, making sure that each banana slice gets a touch of honey. The aroma of the sticky-sweet honey meets with his nose and memories pop into his mind similar to earlier in the morning, but this time they are about being on the farm. His Uncle Roger tended to the bees and taught him how to harvest honey once the combs in the frame were full.

Gareth shakes off the refection and places the other piece of toast on top of the sandwich and uses the butter knife to cut it in half. Just as he puts the plate in front of Alysia's chair, the next batch of bread pops out of the toaster. He makes another sandwich for himself and sits down at the table. "It must be pretty good. You're almost halfway done." he says.

"It's yummy. Can we have this again?"

"Sure." Gareth bites into his sandwich. The flavor of honey intermingles with the banana and creamy peanut butter. His memory goes back to his Uncle Roger. He made Gareth wear full protective gear to keep from being stung by the bees, but he wore only a hat with a screen. Uncle Roger was famous in town, he didn't even wear gloves when removing the frames from the hive.

"See, you have to be calm and peaceful when you approach the bees. It's sunny and warm out today, so they're pretty happy. They just want to go back to what they do," said Uncle Roger. He lifted the lid off the hive and grabbed the smoker to puff some smoke around the box. "The smoke keeps them from communicating with each other and pushes them down in the hive. It calms them and takes their focus off us."

Gareth remained silent, watching him work his magic a few steps away. Uncle Roger continued his instruction. "As you know, we only take honey from the top box, that's called the honey super. It has the excess honey the bees don't need to survive the winter." The bees were climbing on the top of the frames and buzzing all around Uncle Roger, but he didn't mind, he went about his work.

"We use this tool, called the hive tool, to remove excess wax and pry the frame out of the box," he said. After demonstrating, he pulled out a frame, and the bees weren't swarming him at all. He held the frame up in the air. "Look, this one is entirely capped with wax and it's heavy. Lots of honey in here." He completed this many times until they headed back to the barn with the harvest.

Back at the barn, Uncle Roger said, "Here's your job. Take each frame and cut off the wax caps that keep the honey in the compartments. To do that, you use a comb knife." He takes the knife and slices the layer of wax that lies on top of the frame and honeycomb. "Be sure to let the wax fall into the bucket. We'll filter out any honey and keep the wax for other uses. Now you give it a try."

Abruptly returning to the present, Gareth stops chewing on the sandwich. "*The honeycomb. It's a six-sided hexagon,*" he thinks. Pieces of the basic honeycomb shape move in his mind until layers overlap and change colors. "*That makes convertible workstations of the perfect proportions. Three hexagonal individual workstations share one hexagonal table, so if you raise the three dividers that separate the workstations, they become one collaborative work area. We could repeat this same pattern in groups of three to create a flexible workspace.*"

"Dad? Are you even listening to me?"

Pulled completely out of his mind, he turns and looks at Alysia who has finished her breakfast minus a few crusts that lay on her plate. "I'm sorry. Something distracted me for a minute. What were you saying?"

"I was asking, do you want to make a collage today? You said we would."

After thinking a moment while chewing the bite in his mouth and swallowing, he says, "Sure, that's a fantastic idea, but I have to do some things around the house first. Do we have all the supplies? Paper, tissue paper and glue?"

"Yes, I have a stockpile. I can't wait! I'm finished eating. Can I go play in my fort now?"

"Yes, okay. Clear-off your plate first."

Alysia jumps-up, scrapes the crusts off the plate into the garbage and rinses it in the sink. As soon as Gareth hears the clink of the plate on the counter, she cruises out of the kitchen, headed down the hall to her fort.

Gareth gets a load of cloths in the washing machine before cleaning-up the kitchen. By the time he finishes the dishes, the washer buzzes. He puts the wet clothes into the dryer and starts another load in the washer. The cloudy morning turned into a drizzly day so, he continues with housework, starting with giving the living room a quick dusting and vacuum. The cycle of housework and switching loads of laundry continues until he's folding the last load of clean cloths while sitting on the couch.

Alysia runs into the living room. "What are you doing? Is it collage time yet?"

"Good timing. The basket there is all your cloths." He nods toward a laundry basket that's full of fresh smelling and neatly folded cloths. "Put them away and we'll get everything together to do some crafting."

"All right!" She grabs the basket and wobbles as she carries it down the hallway.

Pretty soon they are camped out on the living room floor with white paper sheets, colored tissue paper, and glue sticks. Gareth watches as Alysia takes tissue paper squares and tears them into smaller pieces. She takes the pieces and tosses them up, so they land in a scatter, then she selectively picks pieces to glue on the white paper. She works on the outline, and it looks like she is making an evergreen tree of some type. Once she is engrossed in her project, he crawls over to his bag sitting by the front door and flings it open. He pulls out a drawing pencil and a ruler. He draws three hexagons in a honeycomb pattern that would be the walls of the workstations.

"Humm, I think I will use purple tissue paper for mine," he says.

"Pretty, I like purple," replies Alysia while still making progress on her tree.

Gareth draws a single hexagon the same size as the others while managing not to tear the thin tissue paper and uses scissors to bring the shape to life. Then he places the tissue hexagon on top of the three he drew on the white paper. He rotates the purple tissue shape that represents the tabletop until each of the white hexagons has their own side for a working table. He looks at it, satisfied. It's as he figured. He grabs a glue stick and runs the glue across the entire surface of the tissue shape. By placing the tissue shape back into place, it bonds with the white paper.

He leans back on the couch and grabs the remote. This catches Alysia's attention. "What are you doing? Are you done already?"

"Mine's done!" He holds it up for inspection.

Alysia stares at it and tilts her head to the side. "It's pretty simple."

"Oh, you think so?" He teases.

She looks at a little longer. "It looks like a flower."

Gareth turns the paper so he can glance at the figure again. "Your right. I guess it does."

"Do you want to help me finish mine?" she asks.

"No, keep going! You have an original work of art started."

"Okay. I was thinking about adding mountains or something in the background."

"That sounds like a great idea."

Alysia turns her attention back to her collage and Gareth flicks on the TV. It's still on the public television station and there is a small hut with a bird hopping around it, making all kinds of bird sounds. Just as his thumb is ready to start channel surfing, Alysia says, "I saw this one before, this is cool too. I think it's called a bowerbird."

"Since you saw it before, let's see what else is on," says Gareth in an encouraging tone.

"No, just wait until after this part. He decorates the outside of his house."

"What?"

"Just watch," she replies.

Gareth relaxes and watches as the bird flies away, returning with orange trumpet flowers. The bird does this again and starts arranging them in piles. The narrator on the program describes how the bird is decorating outside his giant bower and calling to attract a female. They further elaborate, this bird seems to favor red and orange colors. They show the bird creating another pile of saucer-shaped red flowers outside of the opening to the bower.

"First there are dancing birds and now we have decorating birds. Who knew?" questions Gareth, mostly talking to himself.

"See, I *told you* it's cool," says Alysia.

Gareth pulls out his parental tone. "All right." He goes back to watching the nature show for a couple of minutes. Then he remembers. "Hey, I forgot to tell you. We're going to Tree Side Village tomorrow."

"What for?" asks Alysia.

"Oh, they have a cool Recreation Center where you can play with all the other kids. I'm sure they have a lot of fun things to do. Aunt Emma will be around, so you'll see her for a little while."

"I like the sound of that."

"Good. But we have to get up and get an early move on for a Sunday. You know what that means…"

"I do?" Alysia asks in a coy tone.

"You do. It means getting to bed at a reasonable time tonight. We can still order take out for dinner, but we'll have to skip the late-night weekend movie. Besides, it could be a long day."

⁂

Gareth lets out a deep breath after he walks out of Alysia's bedroom, leaving the door ajar. It took one minor battle, making sure he turned the nightlight on, nestling Curly the poodle, her favorite stuffed animal at her side, and completing a bedtime story until she was struggling to keep her eyes open. Outside the kitchen, he looks at the refrigerator and does something he hasn't for a very long time. He opens the door and rummages through its contents.

"I think there's a beer back here somewhere," Gareth murmurs out loud. He finds a bottle of pale ale from Growler Microbrewery. He takes it out, opens it with a bottle opener and pours it into a beer glass. The tiny bubbles raise-up the middle and a thin layer of foam coats the top. He brings the glass up to his nose and inhales the smell of fruity hops. While leaving the living room mostly dark, he plops down on the couch, unbuttons the top three buttons on his shirt, rests one foot on the coffee table and turns the TV back on being quick to turn down the volume. He picks a random basketball game and leans back. The muscles in his shoulders and lower back relax as he sinks into the cushions, sipping the ale.

The game ends, and he lifts himself out of the couch. He feels a little heavy as he patters down the hallway, so he quickly gets into his pajamas and crashes into bed. The soft mattress cradles him underneath and the fluffy comforter covers him on top. By tucking his favorite pillow under his head, a roll forms under his neck, and sleep quickly takes over.

Amid deep sleep, he has a short but unforgettable dream. He's standing in a room that is all black with subtle lighting. Suddenly a woman in a flowing white dress is walking towards him. He can't make out her face at first, but he notices her distinct outline, and he knows. She walks closer and he can see the slope of her cheeks and curve of her nose. "Caitlin, I love you so much, but you're not here," he says.

An unmistakable wave of love passes through him. She keeps walking closer and closer until she stands in front of him, looking into his eyes.

He wants to touch her face, but he's paralyzed and can't move a muscle.

She reaches out her hand while saying, "It is okay." Her hand draws closer to him. "You already know," she says. Her finger touches his chest.

A golden light surrounds them at the same time a burst of warmth and pleasure spreads from her finger into his entire chest.

Everything in the room dims and the scene shifts. He looks above him and there are colorful birds and flowers floating through the air. They are moving in random circular patterns and glitter when light coming from somewhere reflects off their surface. The floating birds and flowers spin faster and faster until his stomach churns so hard he abruptly wakes-up.

Gareth props himself on his elbow for a moment. He can feel his heart knocking on his chest and his breath flowing in and out of his lungs. His stomach has a queasy knot that doesn't want to let go. When he lies back down, the heat on the pillow and from under the covers radiates into the surrounding air. Once he feels centered enough, he gets up and retrieves a glass of water from the kitchen. After finishing half the glass, he gets back into bed, and lays there for almost an hour before sinking back into deep sleep.

Spiritual Practice

Gareth sluggishly pulls off the comforter and swings his legs to the side of the bed until his feet meet the floor. The partially finished glass of water still sits on the nightstand and he takes it with him to the kitchen.

Without hesitation, he gets the little coffee maker brewing. He takes his first sip and closes his eyes. Alysia trots into the kitchen, still carrying Curly the poodle. She sits at the table and squints her sleepy eyes at him. "Are we having breakfast yet?"

Gareth leans back against the counter and takes another sip of coffee. Once he is more awake, he replies, "How about, you have a glass of milk, and we grab breakfast at the diner on the way out of town?"

"Oh yummy! Can I have pancakes?"

"Sure." Gareth gets a glass and sets it on the table. He pulls the milk out of the refrigerator and fills the glass. "Great, it's a plan. Finish your milk before you get dressed." He has a few more sips of his coffee that has cooled to the perfect drinking temperature. "I'm going to take a shower."

"Okay. I'll wear my pink flower shirt with jeans today," chirps Alysia, and she takes a couple of hearty drinks of milk.

"Excellent choice." Gareth sets his cup down on the counter before making his way to the bathroom. He steps into a hot shower and takes his time. Once he finishes his shower, he shaves and gives his hair a little style.

He buttons up his shirt before walking into the hallway and finds Alysia playing in her bedroom. The fort has gotten saggy, and a little disheveled. But she dressed and got her hair nicely brushed. "Very good! Go ahead, wash your face, and brush your teeth so we can get going."

"Oh yah, pancakes. I forgot." Alysia drops her toys and skittles to the bathroom.

Gareth shakes his head a little. "*Again, lost in her imagination, without a care in the world. She even forgot about pancakes.*"

They step outside into the sunny morning. After breakfast, it takes about twelve minutes to get to Tree Side Village. Gareth pulls into the Community Center parking lot and finds a place to park. He looks at the time. "We made it with three minutes to spare."

They get out of the car and immediately Alysia sees Emma standing on the sidewalk in front of the building. Alysia waves and yells, "Hi Aunt Emma!"

"Please don't run in front of traffic." Gareth worries out loud and grabs her hand.

They meet Emma and the three of them walk into the Community Center. "The Recreation Area is down this way," says Emma. Gareth and Alysia follow as Emma leads the way. Emma stops at the door. "I'll let you two get things settled."

Gareth stops to scan the inside of the center. It's much larger than he imagined. There are children of all different ages playing in groups. Some are in an area with a pretend grocery store made of toy props while others are at tables coloring, drawing, or playing board games. Then some are participating in a group activity lead by a staff member. He sees that in all areas, staff are circulating around and interacting with the children. Everything meets his approval, and he lets Alysia tug him by the hand to the reception table.

"Hello, my name is Julie, and this is Shrishi," says the young woman sitting at the table. "How can we help you?"

"Hi. I'm Gareth, and this is my daughter, Alysia. Alysia is here to play while I attend the Spiritual Practices Service down the hall."

"Welcome. We are glad to have you both at our Community Center," says Julie. "Is this your first time here?"

"Yes, we're here with Emma."

"Oh yes, Emma. She's such a giving person." Julie smiles. "Okay, so we give all our participants in the Rec Center a wrist band and one that matches to the person who will pick them up later." She slides two wrist bands across the table to Gareth.

Once Gareth gets the wristbands on himself and Alysia, Julie leans a little over the table. "Alysia, this is Shrishi. She will show you around and then you can pick which group you would like to join."

Julie sits back up and looks at Gareth. "She'll be fine. See you after services."

"Thank you," he says before joining Emma outside the door. It's a short walk down the hallway to the community room.

"Here we are. It sounds like we're having live music today," says Emma.

Gareth walks into the room behind Emma. A guitarist is playing uplifting music, and groups of people are having conversations. "Wait." Gareth puts his hand gently on Emma's arm. "Your leader is a woman?"

Emma tilts her head. "What? You mean Mikita? Yes, she's a woman."

"I guess I was just…"

"Expecting an old man with wrinkly skin?"

Gareth laughs and looks down at the ground while bobbing his head.

Emma leans closer and whispers, "Her father just retired from giving public services. Mikita has been under his study since she was very young. I heard she has even journeyed to the east."

He barely hears what Emma is saying since he is focused on Mikita while she talks to other participants. She has a warm smile, and her long hair softly flows with her every motion. "She is so different," he absently says out loud.

"Well, we should say hello. I'll introduce you. She usually seeks out every new person to greet them, anyway."

Gareth's mind is blank as he follows Emma. "Mikita, how nice to see you," Emma says as she approaches her. "And you're wearing your dressy linens today. Lovely."

Mikita gives Emma a slight bow. "It's so nice to see you as well. Thank you, I thought I would wear them in honor of spring. You know, the embroidered flowers and all." Mikita says with a smile and a slight blush rising up her cheeks.

Emma turns towards Gareth before saying, "Let me introduce you. This is Gareth. He's joining me today for services."

He hears his name and becomes more tuned into what Emma is saying. He makes eye contact with Mikita. "Very nice to meet you."

She gives Gareth a slight bow. "We're glad you're here to join us."

"Thank you. It looks like you have a good-sized group here."

"It varies, but yes, I guess you're right. Please let me know if you need anything. When we have music, we usually spend some time socializing before starting structured activities. There are water bottles on the table in case you need to hydrate."

"Thanks again. I will let you get back to greeting everyone." Gareth turns to where Emma was standing and sees that she has wandered off to visit with others. Not sure where to head, he walks towards the table to get a water bottle. He takes a bottle, removes the top, and has a few drinks. Emma calls out to him, "Gareth, come over and meet Ellen."

He walks over to join Emma and the other woman. "Hello," he says.

"Gareth, this is Ellen. She owns the art gallery in town," says Emma.

"Nice to meet you, Ellen. An art gallery, how great. My daughter loves making art."

"It's always good to hear about young aspiring artists," Ellen says, followed by a cheerful laugh.

"She's definitely still in the aspiring stage." Gareth jokes back. "How long has your gallery been open?"

"Oh, not too long. We're just approaching a year now. You should come by and see it, bring your daughter, I'm sure it would inspire her."

"That sounds like a great idea."

Thomas approaches the group. He sees Gareth and sticks out his hand. "Hello, I'm Thomas, Ellen's husband."

Gareth accepts his firm handshake. "Great to meet you, I'm Gareth."

Ellen looks at Thomas. "We were just talking about the gallery."

Thomas puts his arm around Ellen and looks at Gareth. "Oh yah, it's fantastic!" His smile broadens. "It's opened this afternoon. You should stop by and have a look."

Gareth gestures with his water bottle in Ellen's direction. "That's what Ellen was just saying. I look forward to seeing everything."

Ellen tugs on Thomas's hand that is dangling over her shoulder. "Honey, there's Mr. Reedy. We should ask him about doing the landscaping around the shop. Did you see his yard? It's fantastic."

Thomas turns his attention to Ellen. "Sure, let's go talk to him. Maybe we can have him take care of landscaping at the house too."

"Okay." Ellen giggles and leans into Thomas.

Gareth watches the couple navigate to different parts of the room. And again, Emma has wandered off to take part in other conversations. He surveys the activity going on and a young man is pulling votive candles out of a box and putting them into glass holders. He allows himself to be drawn towards the table. As he arrives at the young man's side, he says, "Hi. I'm Gareth. Would you like some help?"

The young man pauses and says, "I'm Alan. Yah, sure, if you want to take the glass holders out of that box and spread them on the table, that would be cool."

"Got it. Consider it done." Gareth completes the task and Alan hands him candles to place in the holders that are closer to where Gareth is standing. The guitar music continues to fill the air along with the distinct scents of the candles. Gareth asks, "So, Alan, what do you like to do? Are you into any sports or anything?"

Alan pauses what he is doing again and looks at Gareth. "I wasn't sure, but I take it you haven't lived here long. I'm into baseball."

"No, I don't live here at all. I'm here with Emma." Gareth chuckles and points his chin in the direction where she is talking with other folks.

"Oh yah, Emma's nice."

Gareth uses the sentiment of the woman at the Rec Center to agree. "Yes, she is very giving." After placing a couple more candles into the holders, he says, "So you're into baseball?"

Alan bounces his head up and down. "Yah, I just started playing for the university this past fall. I'm home on spring break."

"That's impressive. Good for you."

"Thanks. It's going really well."

"That's great. I like baseball, but I'm more of a basketball man myself," says Gareth.

"Basketball is its own, fast paced sport. It reminds me of hockey. I used to play on a hockey team." Alan puts an empty box on the table. "The candles are for today's meditation."

Mikita appears among the clusters of people socializing. She looks at Gareth, then turns to Alan. "Are we ready?"

"Yah, I think so," replies Alan.

"We were just talking about sports," says Gareth.

Mikita grows a small smile. "I'm glad you two met." She looks over the candle arrangements on the table. "Excellent. Thank you so much. I'll get the next activities started."

Gareth watches as Mikita walks to the front of the room. Without thinking he says out loud, "You have an interesting spiritual leader."

Alan looks at her and turns back to Gareth. "Yah, she told me she prefers to be called a spiritual guide." He bobs his head. "She's super observant and deep. I like her a lot."

"I'm getting it." Gareth spies Emma and steps away so he can join her. "Good luck with everything at the university."

The guitar music ends as Mikita turns to face everyone. She opens by saying, "Hello everyone. How wonderful we are together again. We went a little over on the visitation time, so let's get started." She lets the group shift their attention to her. "Everyone get a mat, and candle from the table. Let's line-up in rows with plenty of space. We will use the candle during meditation today."

The group bustles around, gathering the items and getting settled on their mats under Mikita's watchful eye. Once things quiet down, she says, "Great. Before starting this week's meditation, let's take some time to share experiences with the assignment over the week. We had talked about using mindfulness to become conscious of one thing that we hadn't noticed before during our daily activities. It could be anything, something small at home, on our commute or in the nature that surrounds us. I got to chat with Anya this morning and she kindly agreed to share her story to get us started." She extends her hand towards Anya, then sits on her mat.

Anya smiles at everyone. "Well, I made my regular walk in the neighborhood into a mindfulness walk. I got to a spot where there are a bunch of trees and saw a robin flying in and out of a particular evergreen tree. I stopped and watched, and there were two robins flying in and out from the same spot. There must be a nest in the tree. All the times I passed it this spring, I never noticed that before."

"Isn't that nice?" Mikita grasps her hands together. And a few participants utter reinforcements to the sentiment. "So much activity can go on around us and sometimes we don't even notice."

Gareth thinks about his walk around the city and finding the open-air market until Mr. Reedy offers, "I'll go."

"Wonderful. Please share," says Mikita.

"Mine's a little different. I was sitting in my recliner where I sit every day and paid special attention to what was in the room. We have a small bookcase, and all the books were organized and a lamp I didn't remember was sitting on top. I asked my wife when she cleaned-up the bookcase and got a new lamp. She said about two months ago."

Mr. Reedy and the participants laugh. Still smiling, Mikita nods her head. "Sometimes we don't notice things that are *very* close to home. Okay, how about one more?"

"I'll share," says Emma.

"Great. Thank you, Emma," says Mikita.

"Well, I pick up my niece every school day. While I was waiting for her, I was mindful of the school. It didn't take long until I spied a full-size blow-up astronaut in the window on the second floor of the building. He had a big smile, and his hand was waving at everyone. I don't know how long it's been there…"

Emma and the group light heartedly laugh.

Never losing her smile, Mikita says, "You never know where you can notice someone with a smile and a greeting. Thank you, everyone. It sounds like you made the most out of the task."

Mikita pauses a moment before continuing. "Let's move on to today's meditation. We will grow on the work we started in mindfulness and think about focus. You each have a candle, place it in front of you so you can look at it comfortably." She demonstrates with her candle and waits for everyone to get situated.

"Alan will hand a candle lighter to those of you on the end of the rows. Light your candle and pass the lighter down. I'm going to close the blinds a little, so we don't hurt our eyes," says Mikita. She rises and fixes the blinds. Then she walks back towards the group with silent steps. "I know some of you have done similar meditations, but we'll still go through this as a group." She softens her voice and slows the pace of her words. "Everyone is comfortable and in a basic meditation posture. We feel ourselves grounded to the floor and the earth below us." After a moment of silence she says, "Now we will gaze lightly at the flame while relaxing and allowing it to become the center of our attention."

Gareth can hear Mikita's voice change as she slowly walks around the perimeter of the room. "Good. If you're straining, just shift your gaze to looking at the candle holder and observe how the light reflects on the glass. When you're comfortable again, go back to focusing on the flame." She takes a few more steps. "As it becomes the center of your attention, and everything around it disappears, some of you will experience a sense of connection or oneness with the flame."

Mikita returns to the front of the room, sits on her mat, and joins the group in the meditation. Silence and a peaceful energy fill the space.

Gareth relaxes and allows himself to sink into the meditation. Soon, everything around the flame disappears. It feels like only a few minutes passed when the bell on the meditation alarm rings.

After the tone fades, Mikita instructs, "At the first bell, we pull ourselves away from the flame." A few minutes later, the meditation bell rings again. "We are becoming more aware of the room and the world around us, and we refocus on being connected with the floor and earth." A minute later, the bell rings for a last time. "And once we are grounded, we are complete with the meditation."

Gareth stretches his torso and looks up to see Mikita diligently scanning the room. Everyone sits quietly until she addresses the group by asking, "How was that? How does everyone feel?"

The group responds positively and most everyone nod their heads. "Would anyone like to share how that was for them?" Mikita probes further.

Gareth listens as members of the group share their experiences and reactions. They increase his thoughts about how quickly and comfortably his meditation skills came back to him.

Mikita looks at the clock and raises her eyebrows. "My! We are almost out of time already." She stands up from her mat. "If you would like to continue the exercise over the week, chose a single subject and examine it carefully. Again, your subject can be anything you chose, something at home, you encounter during your normal activities or in nature. Focus on it in a similar way as you did the candle. Take your time and allow yourself to absorb its details. Then reflect on a few words you would use to describe your subject or how the activity felt to you. Sound good?"

The instructions for the exercise take Gareth back to his memory of the honeycomb and the idea about creating convertible workstations. The rest of the participants nod, and some folks quietly make comments among themselves as they stand. He follows everyone else's cues and stands with them as Mikita finishes by saying, "Thank you, for participating. Spiritual practices uplift us, and they also change us. I'm available during the week if you need anything, please reach out. Many blessings." She bows to the group. In response everyone bows back and some reply with words of gratitude.

Emma turns to Gareth. Impatient to know, she asks, "What do you think? Did you enjoy the session?"

"I did. It was good. I forgot how centering it is to do this kind of work."

"I'm so glad! It really lifts my spirits. You know?"

"Yes, I get what you mean," says Gareth.

"I would love to spend more time with you and Alysia today, but I want to get to the outdoor market. Some of the best stands get sold out by noon." She pats Gareth's shoulder. "Tell Alysia I said goodbye and I'll see her tomorrow."

"Sure, of course." Gareth pauses for a few seconds. "Emma, thanks for everything."

"No problem. I enjoy that you and Alysia are part of the family."

"I mean it, thank you for everything," emphasizes Gareth.

Emma looks at him deeply. "You are welcome." She smiles at him before heading for the door.

Strange Connections

As Gareth walks into the Recreation Center, he sees Julie is still at the reception table. "Hello, I'm here to pick up Alysia." He holds his wrist so Julie can see the identification band.

"Absolutely." She cranes her head to survey the group. "Isn't that her over at the grocery store?"

"Yes, that's her."

"Great. One moment, Shrishi just stepped away. I'll go get her."

Gareth watches as Julie talks to Alysia, and they both approach the table. Once Alysia sees him, she picks up speed, leaving Julie behind. Alysia grabs his hand. "Daddy, can't I stay a little longer, please?"

"Well, we should get going. The services I was participating in are finished." He looks at Julie, who is getting comfortable in her chair.

"But I haven't had time to do art stuff!"

Julie gives Gareth a subtle nod, indicating Alysia can stay longer. "Well, I was thinking about walking down Main Street to explore some shops. You can come with me or stay here."

"I'll stay here." Alysia says with enthusiasm.

"All right, but if you want to do artwork, start with that now. When I get back, it will be time to leave," Gareth says in his parental tone.

"See you later." Alysia takes off for the tables where other children are drawing and coloring.

Gareth looks at Julie. "I guess she's staying."

He walks to the exit of the Community Center. Just as he passes the room where services were held, he sees Mikita out of the corner of his eye re-opening the blinds. Without thinking about it, he walks into the room. Once Mikita senses his presence, she stops what she is doing and spins around.

"Oh, hello. I was just putting the room back to the way it was when we got here. How can I help you? Gareth, right?"

"Yes, it's Gareth. Sorry I didn't mean to startle you. I enjoyed the session today. I used to practice all the time, but that was years ago."

"Why did you stop?"

"My daughter, Alysia, was born, and things got a little hectic."

"I see. I noticed your wrist band."

Gareth looks at the band. "Oh yes. She's at the Rec Center."

"I'm glad you enjoyed the service this morning," says Mikita and she stands in the same spot a moment. "Is there something else you wanted to talk about?"

"I guess. I haven't really thought it through or anything, but it surprised me how quickly my meditation skills returned. Anyway, I'm working on an extensive project at work and have had a couple of good ideas but sense my creativity is stuck when it comes to the big picture. I'm wondering if you have any suggestions."

"Yes, I noticed you were well focused during the meditation." She gestures to chairs sitting in the back of the room. "Would you like to sit down?

As they get comfortable in the chairs Mikita asks, "Can you tell me more about what you mean by the big picture? If I understand your goals a little more, I'm better able to assist you."

"I guess I'll just explain. I'm an architect and am working on a proposal for a large building in Rolling Hill. I have a general idea for the building, but something is not right about the concept. It's something I feel but haven't been able to put a finger on what would make it better."

"I see." Mikita absorbs the information. "So, what you seek is inspired creativity."

"Inspired creativity?" asks Gareth.

"Yes, inspired creativity goes beyond problem solving, especially within our current perspective. Inspired creativity is when we widen our perspective to generate novel ideas. It's actually a part of increasing consciousness."

"That seems correct. Ideas about the structure and feeling of the building requires a very broad perspective."

"Indeed. At the same time, be aware that when we widen our perspective, we also come to see ourselves better. It brings us closer to our unique talents. The two combined is not always a simple thing to accomplish."

Gareth fidgets with his hands on his lap and repeatedly nods.

Mikita watches him as she says, "Are you aware of something inside of you? Something that might arise if you attempt to know yourself better?" She lets silence pass for a moment. "You don't have to share, it's only if it feels right."

Gareth looks at Mikita. "No, it's fine to share. It's been more than a few years now. My wife got ill at a young age and passed away. She is no longer with us."

Mikita restrains herself from putting her hand on his shoulder. Instead, she replies with compassion. "That must have been very difficult. I'm very sorry."

"Thank you, but I am ready. I really want to turn the situation around and give more."

Again, silence stretches across the room. Mikita changes the focus of the conversation. "Where did you practice before?"

"In Krane with Jayden," replies Gareth.

"Yes, I don't know Jayden personally, but I heard he's very good." Mikita shifts in her seat. "I offer one-on-one sessions during the week for those who are willing to do the work. It sounds like you might be under a deadline to complete your proposal. I'm available this Tuesday or Wednesday in the afternoon if you are interested."

Gareth squinches his forehead. "But I haven't been a member of your community. Accepting a session seems abrupt."

"It's not abrupt at all. Something drew you here. That's all that matters."

Gareth contemplates before he says, "Okay, Wednesday would give me time to work out the details. How about 3:00?"

"That works with my schedule. Let me get you a card with the address. The session will be at a different location. It's the meditation room where I live." She goes over to her bag sitting by the table and produces a card that she hands to Gareth. "When you arrive, park on the street, then follow the path to the back of the house. I will greet you there."

Gareth accepts the card with a serious smile. "Got it, thanks. Follow the path to the back of the house on Wednesday at 3:00."

Mikita walks back to where her bag is located and looks over her shoulder. "Keep in mind, this will require personal work that will have its own rewards no matter what else happens. There are no guarantees you will succeed in your building proposal. The way of things doesn't work that way."

"I completely understand." Gareth scans the card, puts it in his pocket, and walks to the door. Before leaving he turns back to look at Mikita and slightly bows. "I'm grateful for your time."

"You're welcome. It's my pleasure to be a guide," she manages to say just before he walks out of her line of vision.

Gareth treks down Main Street to explore the area. His pace quickens so that it pulls the quiver in his stomach upwards. As he passes Livingston Drive, he makes a mental note of its location since it's the street on the card Mikita gave to him. He keeps his quick pace and passes different shops. A shop with paintings displayed in the window catches his attention and he enters through the front door where he takes in the variety of artwork. Ellen emerges from the backroom. "Hi Gareth, so glad you came to see the gallery."

"This is impressive. It looks like you have work from different artists displayed."

"Yes, the pieces in the front are mine. The rest are from a variety of local artists. We just put in the mobile sculptures." She looks up at the sculptures hanging from the ceiling. "Aren't they fantastic? Such a significant addition to the collection."

Gareth looks up at the mobiles. They drift and sway. Affected by the breeze that came in with him when he opened the door, some are still rotating in slow circles. "They are nice. Very modern looking." He moves around to examine them further. A couple of them depict birds and flowers made of art glass. He spies a particular one with teal birds, orange flowers, and small prisms that diffuse the light to create spots in a variety of colors around the room.

"Is there a particular type of artwork you like?" asks Ellen.

"No, I like all kinds of creativity. You were right, my daughter would love this place, but she wanted to stay at the Rec Center with the other children." Gareth looks around the room and walks near the front window. "You say these are your work?"

"Yes, that was the start of the gallery." Ellen stands by Gareth and lets out a breath tinged with relief.

"Is your artwork what inspired you to do all this?" he asks.

"Yes, I felt art was what I am meant to be doing alongside supporting other artists."

"Your pieces really pull you in—almost as if they come from another world."

"Thank you, I'll take that as a compliment."

"Absolutely. They're great," says Gareth, but he can't get his mind away from the mobile. He walks back to stand under the one he particularly likes, and it comes to him. It reminds him of the dancing and decorating birds in the documentary scenes he watched with Alysia. Even deeper, it reminds him of his dream last night. He moves to look at the sculpture from another angle. It only takes one more inference from that point. A huge mobile sculpture in the glass covered atrium would be perfect. It's another step to creating an immersive experience for everyone who enters the space.

"You really like that one. It's enchanting, I look forward to seeing them every time I come into the shop." She walks over to the counter. "Let me see. I have the artist's card here. Her name is Suzanne, and she has a studio on the edge of town. I remember now, she said she enjoys spending time in the forest and the Great Mountains for inspiration." Ellen hands the card to Gareth.

Gareth smiles and lets a small chuckle manifest in his throat. He accepts the card from Ellen and puts it in his pocket without removing his gaze from the sculpture. With the front window framing the piece, he examines the angle of the sun to the decorations on the mobile. His mind becomes free to imagine the sun rising and lowering around the elegant wings of the birds and petals of the flowers, along with the colorful diffusion of light from the prisms floating all around a large atrium setting.

With her curiosity heightened Ellen asks, "May I as what it is you do?"

The imagery in his mind is broken and Gareth looks at her. "Who, me? I'm an architect."

"Oh, you're an artist too."

"Yes, I suppose so." He pauses. "Guess what?"

"What's that?" she asks.

"I will take it. I want this one."

"It is true, when you're taken with a piece of art then it's the right one," she says.

A couple of thumps and shifting sounds ruminate from the back room. "Perfect timing, that must be Thomas. Would you like to take it home today?"

"Yes, if that's possible."

"Sure, just one moment." Ellen walks into the backroom.

Gareth wanders around the gallery looking at the other impressive artworks until Thomas comes in carrying a small ladder. He opens the latter to set it up under the mobile and leans to shake Gareth's hand. "Hello again, it seems you found something you like."

Gareth returns the handshake. "Yes, this one. I had no idea I would purchase anything."

"They are neat." Thomas climbs the ladder and in a graceful handoff gives the mobile sculpture to his wife.

Ellen secures the piece and says, "It will take a few minutes to get it into a safe package." She pulls out a box and heavy tissue paper. Thomas closes the ladder and takes it to the backroom.

"I was thinking about getting something for Emma. Do you have any ideas?" asks Gareth.

"Emma? She likes her plants and has that herb garden in her yard. She might like something from the greenhouse. I think they even have gift baskets," Ellen says as she progresses with packaging the mobile sculpture.

"That's a great idea," says Gareth.

Thomas returns and Ellen looks at him. "Do you know if Rudy's Greenhouse still has gift baskets? Gareth is looking for something for Emma."

"It's a good bet. They had them this past week," says Thomas.

"Where is it located?" asks Gareth.

"Just continue down Main Street. Go past Yash's Tailor Shop and it's across the street from the grocery store." Ellen keeps her focus on packaging the artwork. "Almost done here."

They finish the transaction and Ellen says, "You know, you could leave the mobile here and pick it up on your way back. That way you don't have to carry it to the greenhouse."

"Thanks, I will do just that."

Gareth finds Rudy's Greenhouse, and the neatly displayed gift baskets near the front entrance. A sales associate from the store approaches him and asks, "Can I help you find something?"

"Sure. I'm looking for a gift for a family member. She likes houseplants and has an herb garden. Do you have a basket she might like?"

"You're in luck. We just put these together." The associate walks to the display. "These have different things like gardening gloves, a variety of small tools, some of your basic seeds such as basil, chives and dill, and a greenhouse gift card."

"Very nice. One of these will be perfect." Gareth looks over the baskets and picks one he thinks Emma would especially enjoy while the sales associate patiently waits.

"I can take care of you over here," the associate says once Gareth finished his selection.

"Thanks, that was easy enough," says Gareth.

Gareth leaves the store, picks-up his purchase from the gallery and returns to the Community Center. He soaks in the sunshine as he stops at the car and puts the gift basket in the back seat. When he starts to place the mobile sculpture next to the basket, he pauses. "*If Alysia sees this, she will definitely want it in her room. I'll take it to the office for now and give it to her later,*" he thinks, and he places the box securely in the trunk.

Near the entrance of the Community Center, Gareth finds the hallway is quiet until he hears the echo of children's laughter and voices. Inside the Recreation Center, Julie is still faithfully sitting at the reception table.

"Hi Julie. Let's try this again." He chuckles. "I'm here to pick up Alysia."

"Yes." She smiles. "Here is Shrishi now."

"Shrishi, would you gather-up Alysia? I think she is still at the art tables," says Julie.

"Absolutely, one moment," replies Shrishi. Less than a minute later Shrishi returns with Alysia walking alongside.

"Hi Daddy! I did so much neat stuff today and I met a bunch of people," says Alysia.

"That's great. Say thank you and goodbye to Julie and Shrishi now."

As they start the short walk to the car, Alysia turns back. "Thank you. Bye-bye!"

Gareth secures Alysia in her booster seat and hands her Curly to snuggle. They pull out of the Community Center parking lot and Alysia tells him all about the time she had in the Recreation Center. He doesn't even try to get more than a word or two in the conversation. He lets her prattle in excitement until the drone of the car traveling along puts her to sleep. They pull into the drive at home, and she quickly opens her eyes. "Are we home already?" she asks.

"Yes, we're here. You are amazing," he replies.

Moving Forward

Gareth puts his bag down and places the package with the mobile sculpture on his desk. He scans the ceiling until he spies an old hook in the corner behind the desk. It's a little high, but still a good place to hang the mobile. He carefully unpacks the sculpture, slides a stable office chair under the hook and hangs the artwork. After taking a few steps away, he examines it again from different angles.

Lem appears for a morning visit. "Oh man, what's with the new addition to your office?"

"Hi Lem. I found it at an art gallery in Tree Side and was thinking it would be a great model for a full-scale mobile sculpture in a large atrium."

"Now, that's interesting. Let me see." Lem walks into the office and starts his own inspection of the sculpture.

"There isn't much light in here, but the prisms create bits of colored light that reflect off surrounding surfaces," says Gareth.

"I would make sure the reflections from the prisms aren't overwhelming, but on this scale they look good. Of course, we would also want the shape of the mobile complementary to the shape of the space."

"Got it. Those are great points. I have the artist's card in my bag. Maybe she would be interested in making some concept drawings. I can visualize the sculpture in an all-white atrium with furniture that carries on the modern style and colors."

"Absolutely." Lem finishes his inspection. "Did you schedule a meeting with Henry about your proposal for Nova?"

Gareth shuffles around the few papers on his desk. "Not yet, but I will later today."

"Great. Let me know if you need anything," Lem says as he leaves the office.

Gareth gets on his computer and accesses the architectural journals. He finds his favorite one, *Architectural Design* and reviews the most recent edition before searching around about environmentally friendly buildings. After completing a literature review and reading until his brain feels full, he gets up from his desk and stretches.

He heads to Henry's office to schedule a meeting. A few steps away, he spies through the glass walls to the private office area. Henry's assistant, Carol, is working at her desk. When he reaches speaking distance he says, "Hello Carol, how are you?"

"Hi Gareth. I'm well, just putting together some booklets for Mr. Kravin. How can I help you today?"

"I need to schedule a meeting with Mr. Kravin for later this week about the Nova presentation."

"Very good, let me check what he has available." Henry's office door swings open, and he is walking out with Asmee. "Well, you have an excellent handle on the direction of your plans. I'm sure it will impress Nirvaan and the others." He holds his hand in the air indicating her to exit before him, "Let's meet again next week."

"I look forward to it," replies Asmee with a growing smile. She notices Gareth standing at Carol's desk. "Hello Gareth, nice to see you."

Gareth reaches for his pen in his breast pocket but finding it's not there, he straightens his tie before saying, "Good afternoon, Asmee."

Asmee turns to Carol on her way out the door. "I will come back to schedule for next week."

Henry stops to inspect one of the booklets Carol has completed. "These are great, Carol," he says and puts the booklet down. "Gareth, glad you are here; I've been wanting to touch base with you. Are you working on a pitch for Nirvaan and the folks from Nova?"

"Yes, I was just scheduling a meeting with you," replies Gareth.

"Great. Which site are you focusing on?"

"The northwest site outside of the city."

"Great, just great. That's perfect, and that fits your strengths." Henry waves a finger back and forth, pointing from Gareth to Carol. "Get something scheduled before the end of this week," he says, then he returns to his office and closes the door.

"He's been really busy." Carol scans Henry's appointment calendar. "The next available time slots he has are late afternoon on Wednesday."

"Is there anything else? I have a couple of appointments late on Wednesday."

"There's one spot on late Thursday afternoon," says Carol.

"That would be excellent." Gareth returns to his office and pulls out the collage he made of the convertible workstations and opens the architectural modeling software. He works out the dimensions of the hexagon shaped workstations, shared hexagon table and the flexible walls. When he gets the basics completed, he leans back and thinks, "*Well, one piece ready.*" He checks the time, and he needs to get headed home.

⁂

As Gareth pulls into the driveway at the house, he thinks about stopping at the artist's studio on his way to his session with Mikita. Once the car is parked, he grabs his bag and makes his normal trip up the sidewalk and opens the door.

"Hi Daddy!" Alysia runs over and jumps up to get a hug. Gareth hugs her back with equal enthusiasm and sets his bag in its usual spot.

"Aunt Emma said she likes the card I made for her just as much as the gift basket!" says Alysia.

"I bet she does. She probably likes the card even more because it's your artwork."

"She was so happy when she found the present and the card. It was fun! We should do that again."

"I completely agree." Gareth follows Alysia as she runs back to the kitchen. "Hi Emma, I see you found the surprise. We just wanted to do something nice for you."

Emma has a beaming smile, and she spins the gift basket to examine its contents through the cellophane. "Yes, I was very surprised, and the card is precious! I'm going to hang it on my refrigerator."

"Why don't you open the basket now?" asks Gareth.

"No, I'll open it when I get home. I don't want to lose anything," replies Emma.

"Well, okay. Before I forget, I have a question for you. Do you mind if we change the schedule a little on Wednesday? I was wondering if you would pick up Alysia and take her to your house instead of here."

"Sure, that's not a problem. I'd love to have Alysia over," Emma says. "I could make dinner. It would be so nice."

"You don't have to go through all that trouble," says Gareth.

"Please, you know I love to cook. I'll use my fresh herbs and Alysia can help me." Emma looks over at Alysia, who has gotten out her crayons and is enhancing the card. "Alysia, you'll help with dinner, right?"

"Sure, sounds good," Alysia says without taking her eyes off the paper.

"It's all settled. I will take Alysia to my place, and we will have a nice a dinner together before you go home." A smile expands on Emma's face. "Wait a minute, why the change of schedule? I'm in too deep not to ask."

Gareth turns, searches the cupboard for a glass, and fills it with water. He leans back on the counter while drinking it down halfway. He can sense Emma staring at him, waiting for a reply. "I suppose, you'll find out eventually, anyway. I'm going for a session with Mikita."

"A one-on-one session with Mikita? That is news."

"I told her I used to practice here in Krane, and she offered. It's no big deal." Gareth brushes off the bigger picture.

"But it is some kind of deal. She is very good at one-on-one sessions and selective about who she coaches. It's amazing since you're new to the community." Emma's smile gets even bigger.

"We talked a little about how I was new, and she was fine with it."

"I'm really glad for you. Just don't underestimate the value of having one-on-one sessions with her. I've watched how she's been part of changing people's lives." Emma's smile continues to grow until the creases on the side of her eyes appear.

"Stop it, you'll get me nervous," says Gareth.

Emma laughs and walks behind the chair where Alysia is sitting. "I'm going now. Can I have my card?"

Alysia holds up the card. "Here, Aunt Emma. I added more flowers and outlined all the letters."

"Thank you. How beautiful!" Standing behind the chair, she gives Alysia a shoulder hug. She meets eyes with Gareth and her smile returns. "Just when I thought it couldn't get any better."

"Bye-bye Aunt Emma! I'll draw you a picture." At high-speed Alysia retrieves more paper from her room, slides back into her chair and picks out a crayon.

"I would love a picture! See you tomorrow," says Emma.

Gareth sets his glass on the counter. "I'll walk you out and carry the basket to your car."

As they walk to the door, Emma smiles and playfully pokes Gareth in his side with her elbow. He exaggerates a stagger and laughs.

New Places

Gareth leaves work and drives down the highway, heading to Tree Side Village. He takes an earlier exit than usual so he can find Suzanne's art studio. With the artist's card Ellen gave him in his hand, he reads the address and looks for Crossway Avenue. The street creeps up on him, but he navigates the turn and follows the addresses as the road becomes less and less hospitable. Eventually, it turns into a gravel road coated with oil to keep dust from being kicked up by traveling tires. He wonders if he made a wrong turn or something until he approaches a driveway with a small sign on the edge of the road. The sign says "Suzanne Studio" and the address he is looking for is clearly printed across the bottom.

He pulls into the drive, and it leads to an extensive structure that looks like a refurbished barn. The car rocks in all directions as it travels across divots and worn potholes. Another car is parked by the building, and he parks alongside. A sign just like the one by the road, is perched besides stairs that lead to the second floor. "This must be it," he says out loud and he puts the car in park. He flings the strap of the bag over his head and makes his way up the creaky wooden stairs. With the card still in one hand, he knocks on the door and waits for an answer.

Gareth hears steps coming closer, and a woman opens the big wooden door wide enough so she can push the outside screen door open. She's wearing worn coveralls and a hairband that pulls her short hair away from her face. Without much expression she says, "Hello? How can help you?"

"Hello, my name is Gareth, and I was hoping to talk to Suzanne about one of her pieces, a mobile sculpture."

"Hi, I'm Suzanne. Gareth, your name seems familiar…"

"I purchased one of your pieces from Ellen's Gallery over the weekend."

"Oh yes, Ellen let me know you bought *Diamond Birds*. Excellent choice, I like that one too. Did something happen, is everything okay with it? Are you enjoying the piece?"

"Yes, yes. The sculpture is excellent. That's why I came to talk to you. I'm an architect in Rolling Hill and was wondering if you were interested in being part of a building proposal," says Gareth.

Suzanne's face brightens, and she briefly laughs. "Please, come on in. I don't have visitors at the studio very often." She holds the screen door so Gareth can enter the loft.

The vast studio is surprisingly tidy yet full of equipment. There are rows of mobile sculptures drifting and swaying in the air that depict a variety of subjects. The mobiles are decorated with art glass pieces that are birds, feathers, leaves, and some look like clouds. "Wow, this place is great," he says.

"Thanks, I think it was a lucky find. The price was right, there's lots of space, and plenty of natural light." She motions towards the large windows and hay loft doors. She walks to an area with two living room chairs and a well-loved couch. "Please, come sit down. Can I get you something to drink?" She opens a small refrigerator and takes out a bottle of tea for herself. "I have water, tea with lemon and maybe a diet soda."

"Tea would be great." He opens his bag and pulls out a folder he put together. "I'm sorry to just show up unannounced. If this is a bad time for you, I can come back at a time that works for you."

"Are you kidding? Something this interesting? I'm glad you're sparing me days of anticipation to find out what's on your mind." Suzanne sets the bottle of tea on the coffee table. She removes some of her drawings that are scattered across the table and places them on the empty chair. She sits on the edge of the couch across from Gareth and looks at him with eager eyes.

"As I mentioned, I'm an architect who works for Kravin Architecture in Rolling Hill." He hands Suzanne a copy of his business card. "Another company, Nova Investment, is looking to build a combined office space and apartment building. I'll be making a proposal to them in a couple of weeks. Another architect in our office and other architectural firms will also make proposals, so it's not likely this idea will succeed. It's a very competitive field."

"So, it's like a grant proposal," says Suzanne.

Gareth reviews the comparison in his mind. "Yes, just like a grant proposal but only one person gets funded, or the investors can move on to an expanded pool of architecture firms."

"Understood. So, what do you want from me?"

"In the building I'm designing, there will be a large atrium and my goal is to make it an immersive experience." He slides a copy of the concept drawing of the atrium he created closer to Suzanne. "One thing the client is asking for is a building that creates a community. It should also reflect the city and the Great Mountains that surround the area. That's where your artwork connects into the picture."

He looks at Suzanne who is intently examining the drawing of the atrium. She has slid closer to the edge of the couch with her knees far apart and an elbow propped on each knee.

"I really liked *Dimond Birds,* because of all the elements, the birds, flowers and especially the prisms. Did you make a sketch before you created the sculpture that we could look at?"

"Sure, sure. I have a sketch somewhere." Suzanne abruptly gets up from the couch. "Let's see, I sent it to Ellen's, so it should be in the file cabinet." She rummages through the cabinet across from the sitting area. "Yes, here." She pulls out a folder and lays the sketch on the table.

Gareth looks it over. "Perfect. Our interior expert said the scale of the prisms to the rest of the elements looked good."

"How big of a mobile are we talking?" asks Suzanne.

Gareth rubs his hands on the tops of his thighs before pulling out another sheet with specifics about the sculpture and slides it over to Suzanne. "Right now, I am thinking approximately fifty feet long by twenty feet wide, with a stabilizing weight at the bottom. It would also be a sculpture that would complement a square space."

He watches Suzanne, who returns to her previous posture except she has one hand covering her mouth.

She scans her workspace. "I don't have the equipment to make something that huge."

"That gets to what else I need from you. It would be a proposal of your own. Two or three sketches of different mobile sculptures that fit the perimeters we just spoke about and a budget. If you need to rent a larger kiln or workspace, then add it to a budget along with a salary for your time, materials you'll need, and so forth. You can keep the drawing of the atrium and specifics about the sculpture. Your proposal doesn't have to be perfect, just do the best you can with what we have right now."

"Are you serious?"

"Absolutely." Gareth straightens his posture and allows a pause to release the edgy energy that has built. "One last thing I will mention is there's freedom to be creative. Add additional elements, change elements around from how they are placed in *Dimond Birds*. Create an idea that reflects the best possible artwork for the space and the people that would be part of the community."

"I understand it's a three-point shot thrown just before the buzzer but getting something like this is what every artist dreams about happening."

"Now, you're speaking my language." He smiles, then shifts in the chair.

Suzanne rises from the couch and puts her hands in the side pockets of her coveralls. She walks across the long part of the studio and stands by the open hay loft doors. Gareth packs the remaining paperwork. He leans back in the chair and opens the bottle of tea before taking a few swigs then sets it down on the coffee table. With nothing else to do, he leans over and fidgets with the papers in his bag until she returns.

"Sure, sure. I will put together a proposal," says Suzanne.

"That's excellent. How long do you think it will take?"

"About a week, maybe a little less. It depends how quickly my ideas flow."

"You're right on track. A realistic budget is important but at this stage of the game, the ideas for the artwork and the sketches are primary."

"I'm glad you've said as much." She remains standing with the hands in the pockets of her coveralls.

Gareth stands from the couch and looks at the sketch of *Dimond Birds*. "One last thing. I'm meeting with my boss at the end of this week. Can I take the sketch with me?" Silence penetrates the conversation, so he continues by saying, "It would be very helpful. I will keep safe track of it and return it when I come to pick up your proposal next week."

Suzanne goes to the area by the file cabinet and retrieves a thick paper sleeve. She slides the sketch into the sleeve and hands it to him.

Gareth accepts the sleeve and smiles. "Thank you. I look forward to seeing your proposal. In the meantime, if you have questions, you have my card with all my contact information."

"Sure, sure. This has been the most interesting business conversation I've had in a long time." She laughs with a pleasing rhythm as she extends her hand.

Gareth's body grows lighter as he accepts her handshake. "It has been interesting." He makes his way to the doorway with Suzanne and pushes the screen door. He turns back to her and says, "Thank you for your time, for everything."

"You're welcome," she replies and nods her head.

Gareth climbs down the stairs and gets into his car. "*One more piece in place*," he thinks before backing out of the parking spot and pulling out the bumpy driveway. He takes the turns to get back on the highway.

This time he takes the exit that leads him to Main Street. He turns down Livingston Avenue and pulls out the address card Mikita gave him. Just like finding the Studio, he follows the address numbers down the residential street. He finds the house at the end of the street and parks the car. "This must be it," he says out loud for the second time today. He reaches for his bag but contemplates it might be better to leave it in the car. Instead, he grabs the light jacket sitting on the passenger seat.

Gareth walks to the back of the house. The back yard is lined with trees that are bursting with young leaves and a late afternoon breeze that fills the nooks and crannies. There are decorative stone circles that make a path to the steps of a deck. As he reaches the top of the steps, he sees motion inside of the screen doors. Mikita opens the screen. "Hello Gareth. It's good to see you again."

Gareth slightly bows. "Nice to see you as well."

"Please come in." Mikita moves aside so he can enter the meditation room.

Gareth observers her fluid motions as she walks further into the space. She faces him and says, "Are you ready?"

"Yes, I think so," he replies.

"Would you like to be inside or outside? It's where you will be more comfortable."

"I wouldn't mind being outside. Your deck is very nice."

"Wonderful." Mikita walks over to a bin and pulls out a mat that she hands to Gareth.

Gareth accepts the mat and walks out onto the deck. He takes in the woods and places his mat next to the empty one. Then he sits crossed-legged and waits for Mikita. Her footsteps behind him are barely audible, and she settles on her mat.

"I thought today we would do something fun, a more playful meditation."

"More fun?"

"Yes, part of inspired creativity involves going outside of our comfort zone. When we widen our perspective and put together novel ideas, it's something that defies what we encounter every day," replies Mikita.

"What did you have in mind?"

"We will start by reading a passage. For the meditation, we'll visualize practicing a profession that we would never consider and really don't have the ability for, but in our scenario, we are excellent at the skills involved. Then we will relax the mind, letting go of any thoughts and slowly come out of the meditation."

"Okay, but I haven't done anything like that before..."

"Good then, the experience itself will fit with the point of the activity." Mikita smiles. "What are you going to be? Try to think of something different from anything you have done, something fun."

Gareth thinks about sports. "I will be a world class ballet dancer." He laughs.

"And I will be a race car driver." Mikita laughs with him but quickly regains her composure. She produces a large index card. "Here, this is for you. Sorry, for the informal handwriting. We planned this rather quickly. When you are ready, read the passage out loud."

Gareth looks at the card and a smile develops on the corner of the lips when he examines the elegant handwriting. He shifts on the mat to get comfortable before reading, "*Inspired creativity participates in the process of consciousness. In it we gain a wider perspective of the world around us and uncover more about ourselves. This generates novel ideas that fits with the whole at this moment in time yet are unique to us.*"

He takes a breath. "*This process is what binds us to each other and every living thing we encounter.*"

"Excellent. Now we will go ahead with our exercise. Allow any initial thoughts to pass, keep focused on how the passage makes you feel and relax into your imagination."

Gareth begins and enters his imagination. There he sees himself in a white leotard with racy black accents. He makes basic ballet moves on a stage accented by dim lighting. Pretty soon he is completing more complex leaps to a rhythm in his head. This continues until a female dancer crosses the stage. They dance together in a series of intertwined moves that progress into coordinated leaps and lifts.

He hears Mikita's voice instruct, "We now begin to pull away from our imagination."

Gareth imagines completing the last moves with the female dancer as the rhythm fades, and they turn to look in the audience's direction. The unseen audience tosses roses that land all around them while he bows, and she curtseys.

Mikita moves the meditation forward. "We are clearing our mind and allowing it to relax."

Gareth lets the dance scene in his mind fade into darkness. Thoughts jog around his brain.

Mikita reiterates, "As the mind relaxes, allow any thoughts to pass."

The muscles in his body further relax, along with his mind. He sees pieces of silent memories. He remembers studying hard in school and doing the research in his office earlier in the week. Then he remembers visiting architectural sites and talking to Lem about the iconic buildings in the area until the northwest site for the proposed building comes to mind.

Again, Mikita's voice guides the end of the exercise. "We slowly end the meditation by becoming more aware of the deck below our bodies and the forest that surrounds us. When we are ready, we will open our eyes."

Gareth takes his time before opening his eyes. Letting everything come into focus, he takes in a quick breath because enough time has passed that the trees are casting longer shadows. When he turns back to Mikita, he finds she is intently watching him.

"How was that? How do you feel?"

"It was good, I feel centered. I just didn't realize how much time had passed."

"That happens." Mikita smiles and turns back to the trees.

Gareth does the same, and spontaneous words spring out of his mouth. "I need to visit the sight!" He puts his hand on the side of his head. "It's so simple. I haven't been over to that side of the city for years. I need to visit the site for the building, take it in and feel it."

"You know that will be helpful?"

Gareth turns to her and says, "Yes, I'm almost positive and I feel, well, like a kid again."

"Very good. It seems the exercise was a success."

Gareth picks up the card with the passage and hands it back to Mikita.

"No, you keep it, it's for you. You can carry it with you and read it whenever it comes to mind."

"Thank you." He folds the card in half and puts it in his jacket pocket. "What happens next? Can we schedule another session?"

Mikita rocks back and forth, then looks at him with a furrowed brow. "You already have the tools you need to practice on your own and are welcome to community services." She looks back at the trees. "Your skills are quite advanced. I'm not sure what else would guide you further."

"There must be something. I feel so close to, I don't know, being complete." Gareth stops and allows a lengthy silence to generate. "I'm sorry, I shouldn't have pushed. You have been gracious with your time for my benefit."

Mikita remains motionless, looking at the trees, and a breeze floats by so her hair lifts away from the side of her face.

Gareth worries he has offended her in some way, and as he is about to stand, she clears her throat.

"There is one thing," she says and leans over, so they make eye contact. "It would require a large commitment on your part." Mikita rocks back and forth again. "You could go on an exploratory."

"An exploratory?"

"Yes, you would travel to the east. Travel to explore the grasslands and its close neighbor."

"The grasslands? Has anyone really been there? I thought it was just a place made up for children's stories."

"Yes, people have been there, but it would not be a simple journey. It would take an entire day, from sunrise to sunset."

"And would I travel on foot?"

"Yes, on foot. I should also tell you, not only will the exploratory take all day, but you will also need to rest for a day or two after." She raises her knees and slides to the side, so she faces him directly. "By traveling to the unknown, you will uncover some of what is unknown in yourself. You will get to know more about yourself and any creative ideas you harbor."

"That sounds really intense," mumbles Gareth.

"I just wanted to be clear about what it would require on your part. I would prepare a backpack, so you don't have to bring anything except for the card with the passage. You would come here around sunrise, and we would have a session to bless your journey. When you are ready, you would walk from here to the east." Mikita tilts her head slightly to the side. "The choice is completely yours to make. As my father would say, there are no right or wrong answers."

"If I were to agree, when would I go on this exploratory?"

"Usually, it's done without delay, but you must follow the insight from today first and visit the site. If you agree, Friday will work out well."

Gareth places a hand over his mouth, then cups his chin. "Well, I could take Friday off of work and Emma could take Alysia for the weekend," he says to himself.

"How about I give you a moment to think about everything?" Mikita rises and disappears inside the screen doors.

Gareth's thoughts wander back and forth. "*I can work out the logistics. Will it really make a difference to the outcome of the project? It sounds like it would be an adventure. What did I get myself into now?*" He raises his knees and lowers his head.

Mikita returns to her mat, and they sit quietly for a few minutes. Gareth ends the silence. "This is completely crazy. I've never heard of anything like you have suggested, but I will go on the exploratory. I will be here just before sunrise on Friday."

"Very well. I will make the preparations here. In the meantime, try not to think about it too much. If anything should change, you know where to find me."

They stand together and pick up the mats. Gareth follows Mikita as she walks into the meditation room. She opens the bin while they talk about the pleasing evening weather.

Another Step

Gareth starts the car and drives to Emma's house. He's glad it isn't far away from Mikita's because his stomach is rumbling with hunger. He pulls into Emma's driveway and sees her house has been well kept. It also looks like her herb garden has expanded.

He knocks on the door and opens it a crack. "Hello? Emma?"

Alysia hears him and comes running with Emma in tow. "Daddy! Where have you been? It's almost past dinnertime."

"Hi there. Everything took a little longer than expected. I'm so hungry," he says.

"That's good." Alysia grabs his hand and pulls him to the dining room. "Come see!"

Gareth eyes the neatly set table with shining silverware and two vases full of flowers on the side table. "Wow! You two went all out."

Alysia pulls him to one of the chairs. "You sit here."

"Okay. This is a real treat." Gareth smiles. He looks at Emma. "Hi Emma. Has everything gone, okay?"

"Hey Gareth. Yes, we've been having a fantastic time," replies Emma.

"That's great. I wasn't sure if the change in schedule would be disruptive."

"Not at all. Are you ready? Alysia has been very excited."

"Absolutely. Bring on dinner!" He laughs.

Both Emma and Alysia retreat to the kitchen, and Alysia returns with a large bowl of salad greens. Emma supervises as Alysia navigates to set the bowl on the table.

Alysia gets into her chair, then Emma returns to the kitchen. Gareth can hear the oven door closing and noises coming from the kitchen. The aroma of perfectly cooked food floats into the dining room and he gets a good idea what they are having but keeps the thought to himself. Emma comes out and puts the main course on the table.

"Homemade pizza. My absolute favorite. This is a treat," says Gareth.

"We know, but that's not all." Alysia giggles.

Emma returns from the kitchen and places another round tray on the table.

"Another homemade pizza!" Gareth leans back in his chair and laughs again. He leans to Alysia. "Two pizzas. Double the fun."

They all laugh, and Emma takes the chair on the other side of Alysia.

Most of the salad and a good part of the pizzas slowly get devoured as the three of them talk about their day. Once he's finished, Gareth leans back and puts his napkin on his plate. "That was excellent. I'm too full for words."

Alysia mimics his behavior and puts her napkin on her plate then says, "I'm bursting."

Emma gathers dishes from the table and takes them into the kitchen. When she returns, she says with a smile, "Alysia, why don't you help carry these into the kitchen? It will keep you from bursting!"

Alysia climbs off the chair and Emma hands her a handful of dishes. By the second round Alysia is up to her normal speed, running back and forth while prattling and laughing. Once they have cleared most of the table, she asks, "Can I turn on the TV and play with Curly now?"

"Of course, thank you for your help," says Emma.

"You're welcome." Alysia's words fade as she runs to the other room.

Emma looks at Gareth. "I guess it's time to clean up the kitchen."

"Please, let me help you." He follows Emma, and they put away leftovers and rinse the dishes until he leans on the counter. "I have something I wanted to talk to you about."

Emma slows her activity and looks over her shoulder. "Oh, what about?"

"I have a huge favor to ask."

"Really? Did you know this before you got me the gift basket?" She jokes and chuckles.

"I just found this out today. It has to do with my session with Mikita."

"Should I sit down?" Emma turns to look at him and chuckles again.

"Be serious. I need to figure this out."

"Alright, I'll stop joking. Please go on."

"I was wondering if Alysia could stay with you from Thursday after school until the end of the weekend."

"Of course, I would enjoy having her for the weekend. She also would probably like spending some more time at the Children's Recreation Center."

"Yes, she had a great time there and elected to stay while I went into town." Gareth looks away from Emma.

"Well, see that all works out. You know my curiosity is out of sight! All weekend, what will you be doing?"

"Mikita offered to do an all-day session with me, and she also said I should plan on taking it easy for a day or so afterward," replies Gareth.

"I see. Does this have anything to do with the proposal for the new building?"

"Well, yes. I'm still on the same track."

"When is the proposal at work due?"

"I'm not sure exactly sure. Sometime the week after next," he says.

Emma continues cleaning then hands a plastic container to Gareth. "Here, have some leftovers to take home."

He accepts the container and holds it up in air. "Thanks. Why were you wondering when the proposal was due?"

"I was just thinking you might be extra busy at work. Maybe it would be a good idea for Alysia to stay here for the week."

"I couldn't ask that of you. Wouldn't that be a burden?"

Emma puts a couple of containers of dried herbs away and closes the cupboard door with a thump. She turns to look at Gareth again. "Are you kidding? Nonsense. I would love having her here. She fills the house with life and happiness." Emma shifts her body and places a hand on her hip. "It could also be good for you. When is the last time you took a break from being a full-time father?"

Gareth looks at her and his mouth flitches, but no words form. Emma takes the opportunity to finish speaking her thoughts. "Besides, I wouldn't have to watch her every minute she's not in school. She can spend time at the Recreation Center. It could be good for both of you."

"This is an unexpected offer." Gareth hands Emma a cutting board from the counter to put away. "Let's see what Alysia thinks of the idea."

Gareth walks into the dining room and sits back at the table. Emma follows and picks a chair at the end furthest from him.

"Alysia, come here a minute. Daddy has a question for you."

"Okay, just a second." Alysia walks into the room with Curly tucked close to her side. She sits on the chair closest to Gareth.

"I'm going to be really busy with a project at work, so Aunt Emma and I wanted to know if you would like to stay with her for about a week. Wouldn't that be fun?"

"A week? Without you here?" Alysia puts Curly on the table and leans her head on the stuffed animal's body.

"That's right. You would get to play at the Rec Center like you did last weekend, and she would take you to school during the week."

"That sounds good." She looks at Emma, then back at her father. "Can I bring Curly and all my animals?"

"Well, you can bring Curly and some of your other animals. Don't you want to leave some home with me, so they can keep me company."

"I guess." Alysia turns to look at Emma. "Aunt Emma, can we build a fort?"

"Sure, of course."

Alysia's eyes brighten. "Can we cook some more?"

"Sure, we can cook, plant some seeds so they grow, or do a bunch of crafts. We can do lots of fun stuff," says Emma.

"That sounds even better." Alysia jumps off the chair and runs over to Emma and leans partially on her lap. "I can't wait. It will be fun to stay here awhile."

"I'm overjoyed!" Emma pats Alysia's back.

Alysia looks at Gareth and asks, "Can I go back and play in the living room?"

"Sure, but we have to go soon. Tomorrow is a school day," he replies as Alysia trots back to the other room. He puts the side of his head in his hand and gives it a scratch. "I guess it's settled. I'll get her bag packed and come get her the following week after work."

"It will be great! Now get the most out of the session with Mikita and be the next architect to build in Rolling Hill."

⁂

Instead of heading straight to the office, Gareth drives through Rolling Hill and finds a place to park across the street from the northwest site. He takes a large sketch pad and his favorite thick pencil with him. After walking a full circle around the area, he chooses a spot aside the road and sits on the ground. "*My building still sprawls too much for this site. It should be more compact. It also doesn't complement the buildings in the city very well.*" With the sketch pad on his lap, he opens to a clean page and sketches the outline of the city's skyline and the surrounding mountains.

Then he turns to a fresh page and sketches a modified version of what he had started in the model. He creates a middle building more rectangular and three stories taller than before, making it fifteen stories high. Then on each of the sides he adds two conjoined structures. These would be eleven stories high, and a quarter of the square feet compared to the tallest building. From the vantage point of the sketch, he places one of those structures further back and the other on the other side further forward. Then he works on the lowest of the conjoined structures where the entrances and tunnels to the atrium would be and makes those five stories high. They are half the square feet compared to the tallest building. Although it's not in the sketch, he imagines the side opposite that one would have an entrance facing Great Mountains Park.

He looks over the sketch and the surrounding area multiple times, then uses his finger to blend lines and add shadows. Once finished, he looks at the shadows on the sketch and thinks about where the sun is located. He turns to the sky and scans around the site again. The building is unobstructed by shadows and gets direct sunlight all day. "*Solar panels, of course,*" he thinks. He holds-up the sketch and three of the four terraces of the building would have some southern exposure. "*Instead of green spaces, the roof tops should have solar panels. That's a lot of surface area, it could be enough to power the entire building,*" he calculates in his mind.

Gareth holds his sketch in the air while moving around the site and imagines the building in three dimensions. "*I like it, it's better. It still could use a little something more, but it's way better.*" He walks back to his car, occasionally looking over his shoulder at the site. He even chuckles with excitement just before crossing the street.

⁂

The elevator doors open, and Gareth makes the turns to get to his office. He sees Lem sauntering in his direction, and a smile grows across his face. "Hello Lem. What are you doing?"

"Nothing much. Where have you been?" replies Lem.

"I was inspired and visited the northwest site." Gareth raises the sketch pad. "It's coming together now, which is good because I have a meeting with Henry this afternoon."

"Oh man, you're tearing it up. Can I do anything?" Lem asks, following Gareth to his office.

Gareth tosses the sketch pad on his desk and sets down his bag. "No, I think I'm okay. I just want to put some details in my drawing." Gareth opens the sketch pad and looks at the sketch of the modified building.

Lem steps-up to the desk and snatches the pad before Gareth has a chance to stop him. He looks at the balsa wood model and then the drawing. "This is good, really good. What did you decide about the terraces?"

"Solar panels. The site is far enough from the city and mountains that nothing is obstructing the daylight."

Lem tosses his head back and laughs. "You really are tearing it up!"

Gareth thinks about everything and asks, "I haven't had a meeting like this with Henry before. You know him way better. What does he want to hear about? What should I expect?"

Lem places the sketch pad back on the desk in front of Gareth. "Foremost, he's a businessperson. He'll want to know why what you present is exactly what the client wants and what's the pitch. I would give him the ideas about the building first and this is where he'll be most informative. Then if there's time I would follow up with corresponding ideas about the interior."

"Got it." Gareth nods and looks at the new sketch again.

"I should let you get prepared. I'll be around if you need anything else."

"Thanks as always."

"No problem," says Lem as he exits the office.

Gareth gets comfortable in his chair and pulls his pencil box out of his bag. He picks a thin sketch pencil and puts in details including the entry ways for the open-air spaces. After that it's just a matter of organizing the rest of his materials. He makes it to the private office area a few minutes early.

"Hello Carol. I have a meeting scheduled with Mr. Kravin."

"Hi Gareth. Yes, he's just finishing-up his previous appointment."

Gareth sits on a chair in the office area and flips through the booklet from Nova. He can hear Carol rustling at her desk and answering an occasional phone call.

The door to Henry's office opens, and he escorts a professionally dressed man across the room. Gareth gathers his materials and makes sure he has his silver pen. He looks down and draws in a deep breath as Henry thanks the businessperson for meeting with him and says something about contacting Carol.

Henry turns from the entry way. "Gareth, good to see you. Sorry if I kept you waiting."

"No problem, I was early."

"Well, come on in—let's get the show on the road."

They enter Henry's large, traditionally decorated office and he says, "Have a seat in the sitting area so we have room to spread out your materials."

Gareth sits and sets down the pile of papers. He rubs his thumb on the etchings on his pen. Then slides out the sketch of the proposed building. "I'll just dive-in."

"Please do. Show me what you've got," says Henry.

"Alright, so this is a proposal for Nova's northwest site. It's an asymmetrical design of multiple heights made of steel and glass. The shape would complement the staggered city skyline and the variations of the mountain tops. The roof tops of the building create ample space for solar panels. We need an engineer to do the exact calculations, but it should be enough surface area to power the entire building. The tallest rooftop would have a large glass skylight, allowing sunlight to flow in above a large atrium. This fits with the clients' requests about the building being environmentally conscious, modern, and something that complements the skyline."

Henry picks-up the sketch and looks it over. He rubs the stubble on his face and takes it over to the window. He moves his line of vision from the city and mountains outside of the window back to the sketch a couple of times. After returning to the chair in the sitting area, he says, "Yes, I like it. I see where you are going." He rubs his stubble again. "It just it needs something to put it over the edge. With the solar panels occupying the roof, it may be a brilliant facade or something along those lines."

Gareth puts his hand on the side of his head and gives it a scratch. "Yes, I see what you're saying."

"I'm not totally sure on that part. Keep working on it, it will come. What do have going on around the first floor?"

Gareth explains the plan for creating the sense of community that Nova is expecting, including the restaurant and retail spaces. Then he follows that with the general plans for the atrium and places the sketch of the atrium next to the one of the building followed by the sketch of *Diamond Birds* from Suzanne in a line.

Henry looks everything over. "Great, just great. Have you spoken with Lem about the interior?"

"Yes, and he has given me excellent advice."

"All right. Let's go back to the bigger picture."

"Absolutely," says Gareth.

"I pretty sure that location is zoned for two floors of underground building. Get ahold of the zoning office and make sure. Obviously, underground floors are ideal for parking. Adequate parking included in the building is a real bonus and if it's in the plans, it will take a chunk out of your budget."

Gareth digs his notepad out of the pile and makes a note. "Great. I wasn't thinking about parking yet."

"Now, on the upside, this Nirvaan and Juhi will really like. The houses in the area that have solar panels are still connected with the city's power grid. That way if something happens where the house doesn't have power, they draw from the grid. I'm not talking about some bizarre string of cloudy days; equipment failure is always a possibility." Henry raises a finger. "Here's the attractive part for Nirvaan and Juhi. It works both ways. When the panels produce an excess of power it goes into the grid and the city pays them for the power that is added."

"Got it," says Gareth as he makes another note.

"I've heard at conferences that other cities will make this arrangement with large buildings. Check with the city and the power company if they will consider it for this project. Carol can give you information about a couple of people to contact. If they resist the idea, find out their reasoning and see me right away. No one wants to be the firm or the architect who designs a building with periodic power issues."

"Absolutely. Having that type of arrangement may also cut down on the amount of battery storage that would be appropriate." Gareth grows a smile on his face.

"After that is cleared-up get an engineer to give an approximate calculation on the solar panel production and the power needs of the building before the presentation so you are very clear everything is covered."

"I was also thinking since the projected residents would include people who want to be closer to the mountains, I would contact Great Mountains Park and see how enthusiastic they are about having a space in the building and being a part of the plant life in the atrium."

"By all means. Sometimes those types of relationships can become very strong, especially if we include the key players at the beginning."

Gareth smiles wider and makes another note before looking at Henry.

"That's what I have to address right now. Get what you have about the exterior of the building into modeling software now. Nirvaan is known to be very unpredictable. Pretend he can call the meeting at any time, and you must be ready."

Henry's last words send a wave of lightheadedness through Gareth. He looks down and grips his pen tighter until it passes.

"You're on the right track. Nova is expecting attention to detail, especially for where we are in the process. To them, it says that we are serious about the building we will deliver. Have you thought about the interior office or apartment spaces at all?"

Gareth's mind goes blank for a couple heartbeats. "Yes, well, just that I have developed an idea for convertible workstations as part of flexible offices. For the apartments all I thought was we could offer a variety of luxury layouts, some with expanded kitchens or bathrooms."

"Great. That's plenty for now. Focus on the building and we can meet mid next week. It doesn't have to be long, but let's pin that down. Think of the surroundings and the building as two complementary colors. Together they are pleasing to the eye yet the one lets the other stand out."

Gareth leans back in his chair. "If you don't mind me asking, do you know Nirvaan very well?"

Henry chuckles. "No, I don't mind you asking. I know Nirvaan well on a business level. He's not one to socialize outside of work, if that's what you're thinking. I've been involved in presenting proposals to him on a couple different occasions but haven't been successful in building with Nova."

Gareth smiles. "I was curious about the business aspect. It seemed clear to me that he's interested in a well thought out proposal. He's very focused."

Henry chuckles again. "You got that right." He looks at the clock across the room. "It's the top of the hour." He stands and motions towards the door.

Gareth gets his materials into a neat pile and stands. He follows Henry, who walks quickly to Carol's desk. "Carol, make sure Gareth gets a meeting scheduled with me by the middle of next week. It can be forty-five minutes if there are meetings back-to-back."

"Certainly, Mr. Kravin," says Carol.

"Also give Gareth the contact information for The Public Works Director. I think it's still John Pollow. And the information for Patricia Russell at RH Energy."

Gareth watches Henry walk back into his office.

Carol shifts his attention by saying, "By the middle of next week. Let's see..."

Gareth turns to her and waits for the options. He tries to stay focused but can think of nothing else besides getting back to his office to get organized.

"Oh yes, there is Wednesday afternoon."

"That would be great," replies Gareth.

"Okay, I will put you in at 2:00."

He scribbles the information on his note pad then smiles at Carol.

Carol returns his smile and hands a sheet to Gareth, "Here is the contact information Mr. Kravin mentioned."

He looks over the sheet. "Thank you so much."

In his office, Gareth navigates around his desk and plops into his chair. By the time he finishes a detailed list of tasks and gets the materials organized, it has gotten late. He rushes to pack his bag but remembers Alysia is at Emma's house, so he slows down to think about his session with Mikita the next day. Before leaving, he packs the pencil box and takes a couple of large sketch pads.

MIKITA

Seeking Council

Mikita walks from the deck into the house after her evening meditation. At the same time, her father walks into the meditation room from the hallway. The moment she sees him, her shoulders and chest feel lighter.

"Mikita, your mother just told me you asked her to prepare breakfast before dawn tomorrow," says Kitchwan.

"Yes, I've been wanting to talk to you all day, but we have been on different schedules," replies Mikita.

"Are you going on another exploratory?"

"No, no. Not me. That's what I wanted to talk to you about. I was working with a learner in one-on-one sessions and things quickly evolved. He's very skilled, and it seemed the right thing to send him on an exploratory but I'm having second thoughts it was a wise decision."

"Well, an exploratory is not a simple thing to navigate, and this seems sudden."

"I know." Mikita shakes her head from side-to-side.

"Let's sit a minute."

Mikita follows her father as he walks over to the desk. They get settled in their normal chairs.

"Do you mind me asking, who is the learner?"

"His name is Gareth, and I've worked with him for a short time. He was at services last week and was very calm and peaceful while maintaining a clear mind for the entire focus meditation with the candle. Afterward he approached me about working on his creativity."

"Gareth? I don't know him. Is he from Tree Side?"

"No, he came with Emma." Mikita closes her eyes so tight the bridge of her nose wrinkles. "Anyway, he said he studied in Krane with Jayden for years."

"Oh yes, Jayden. I think he still practices," says Kitchwan.

"Um yes. Like I was saying, he asked me about working on his creativity because he's an architect who is developing a large building proposal for Rolling Hill."

Kitchwan leans back in his chair. "An architect you say?" His eyes flash for a hint of a second to the brass figures.

"Yes, I know." Mikita crosses her arms. "I scheduled a one-on-one session with him and did an imagery meditation, the one where you visualize yourself in a different profession."

"That's an advanced skill. How did he do?"

"That's just it. I picked it because it supports creativity and can be fun. He's well, pretty disciplined." Mikita waves her hand in front of her neck. "He even buttons his shirt all the way to the top." She smiles. "But he did excellent and had an insight shortly afterward."

"That's good. What led you to suggest an exploratory so soon?" Kitchwan continues to probe.

"When I came out of the meditation, I saw the grasslands, tall city buildings and the joining of two hands. After I opened my eyes, an exploratory to the grasslands was the first thing that came to mind. He asked if we would schedule another session and I tried to discourage him all together, but he was persistent."

"It seems you are on the right path. Why are you reconsidering your decision?"

"From what I gather, his journey will be just as much emotional as creative. In our first discussion he shared a life event that he needs to overcome, to accept and leave in the past."

Kitchwan rubs the top of his head. "That's not a concern, really. We all have our own path and to become the person he's striving to be, he will have to face whatever is inside. At least he's aware of the situation."

"I made that clear to him, but what if something goes wrong? There are all kinds of dangers," she says in a rising tone.

"*Mih-keet-ahh*, is there something you're not saying?"

She uses a finger to pick at a splinter on top of the old desk. "It's embarrassing to say, but he distracts me."

"Ah." Kitchwan gently folds his hands together and places them on top of the desk. "What did you instruct him?"

"I told him he would explore the grasslands and its close neighbor. That he should plan on sunrise to sunset. I also gave him a card with a passage about consciousness and creativity to review and bring with him."

"Excellent." Her father allows a comfortable silence to come and go. "Why don't we return to basics and practice some detachment techniques this evening? Then tomorrow early morning I will do a small blessing for the exploratory and remain at the house the rest of the day."

"That does make me feel better." Knowing her father will wait for her response, Mikita takes the time she needs before she says, "Okay, I will continue forward with everything."

"Very good, trust your intuition and in the way of things." Kitchwan stands and gestures to the open space in the meditation room. "Let's get started."

GARETH

The Journey

Gareth wakes up, and it's still dark outside. He lays in bed a few minutes before wondering if it's time to get going yet. Full of energy, he pulls back the comforter just as the alarm beeps. There is a quiver in his stomach, and the early morning hour disorients him. He walks down the hallway and staggers when turning the corner into the kitchen. Once he gets the coffee brewing, he returns to the bedroom to get dressed.

He puts the coffee in a travel mug and sips the dark, hot liquid while he finishes getting ready. As he puts on his jacket, he makes sure he has the card with the passage from Mikita and puts on his hiking boots. He ties up the laces and thinks, "*These haven't been out for a hike in a while.*"

Gareth takes the mug along as he heads out the door and gets into the car. He drives to the edge of town and stops at the diner. There he orders the big plate breakfast, complete with eggs, sausage, toast, and fruit. Without wasting time, he eats most everything before getting back on the highway towards Tree Side.

The traffic is sparse in the early morning hour, allowing his mind to anticipate what the day might be like; all he knew about the grasslands was what he read to Alysia at bedtime. The quiver in his stomach returns so he refocuses on driving and takes the exit that leads to Main Street. When he arrives at Mikita's, he parks in the same place he did during the week. Since he is warm, he takes off his jacket and retrieves the card before getting out of the car. While walking around the house, he notices the sun is halfway above the horizon.

Mikita walks out of the meditation room just as he arrives. She places the mats she has in her hands on the deck and looks at him. "Good morning, how are you?"

"Hello, I'm good. A little nervous, I guess." Gareth puts his hand on his stomach.

Mikita smiles. "Well, we should get started. Come, get comfortable on your mat. Did you bring the passage?"

Gareth sits cross-legged on the mat and centers his weight. "Yes, I have it right here. I read it a few times after I visited the site for the proposed building."

"Good, so you visited the site. Was that helpful?"

"Yes, it was very helpful."

"Excellent. Let's start with the passage. How does it make you feel when you reflect on the times you read it?"

Gareth thinks about reading the passage before their meditation, in the car after the site visit and in his office. "It makes me feel full inside and very centered."

"Good. What else?"

He focuses more. "Well, warm inside of my chest."

"Wonderful. We can start the meditation. Focus on the centered feeling and the warmth in your chest. I will focus on passages to bless your exploratory. Be sure to let me know when you are ready to start the journey to the east."

"Got it. Let you know when I'm ready to go," he says.

Gareth watches as Mikita shifts, raises her chin slightly, and closes her eyes. He hesitates, takes a deep breath, and does the same while recalling the centered feeling and warm sensation in his chest. As expected, a few random thoughts come and go before his mind silences. While holding on to being centered, the warmth in his chest grows. It escalates until it reminds him of the dream he had about Caitlin. It stays at that intensity for a few minutes. Then the warmth expands through his body, down his legs and up to the top of his head. His eyes open. The sun has almost risen, and the musty smell of spring is in the air. Then he notices that since he was there the other day, the spring leaves on the trees have grown larger.

He turns to Mikita and says, "I think I'm ready."

Mikita opens her eyes. "Let me get you the backpack, it has everything you need for your exploratory." She walks into the meditation room and produces a backpack.

He accepts the old but rugged brown backpack. "It has everything I need?"

"Yes, there is something special in the front pocket." She nods in the pocket's direction.

Gareth dips his hand in the compartment and pulls out a basic but sturdy compass. He inspects it and lines it up with the north so he can orientate to what direction is east.

"Perfect. In the main compartment, there are other things you may need like some granola bars, water and a windbreaker."

He puts the compass back in the pocket and makes sure it's secure, then looks at Mikita and slightly bows. "Thank you."

A shadow appears in the meditation room and as it moves closer, Mikita turns and smiles. The screen door opens. "Hello father, this is Gareth." She looks at Gareth. "This is my father, Kitchwan."

Kitchwan steps onto the deck and grows a wide smile. "How good to meet you. I heard a little about you and wanted to share my blessing for your exploratory."

Gareth looks back at Mikita before turning to Kitchwan and bowing his head. "The pleasure is all mine."

"How are you feeling? Doing all right?" asks Kitchwan.

"Yes, doing well, just about to get started."

"Excellent." Kitchwan looks around at the forest, then turns towards Gareth. "What a beautiful day. Be well. Many blessings on your journey."

Again, Gareth bows his head. "Thank you, Kitchwan." He watches as Mikita's father turns and walks back into the house without a sound. Then he slides his arms through the backpack straps and situates it on his back.

"Trust your intuition and in the way of things. Many blessings on your exploratory," says Mikita.

Gareth walks down the stairs of the deck, faces east, and takes the first steps. The queasiness returns to his stomach, but he keeps walking to see what lays ahead. He finds the wooden path that leads into the forest and relaxes. As the forest surrounds him, the height of the trees and dense foliage puts him even more at ease. The wooden path turns into the dirt trail and time slips by until he stops for a drink of water. Before resuming down the trail, he uses the compass to check its direction and his eyebrows raise when he finds it leads directly to the east. "*Very well, continuing forward*," he thinks, and he puts the compass in the backpack.

A short time later, Gareth sees the opening in the forest. Eventually, he can see the golden grass and bright sunlight. Before stepping out of the forest into the grasslands, he takes a minute to readjust the backpack and makes sure everything is secure. He looks around and shields his eyes from the sunlight. Once his eyes adjust, he takes in the knee-high rustling grass, sparse trees in the distance, and vastness that surrounds him. In the distance he also sees, a herd of small animals are moving across the grass, headed in his general direction. "*Those must be antelope. This place is amazing.*"

While he walks, he keeps his eyes on the herd of antelope. They stop to graze in small groups, yet over time the entire herd inches forward. He hears a voice say, "Hello." And his feet become glued to the ground. His eyes dart from the herd to looking in front of him. He sees an antelope not ten steps away standing on the trail. He gets lightheaded and leans over.

"Are you okay?" asks the antelope.

Gareth looks up at the antelope and takes a step back. No words form in his mouth. The antelope walks around in a circle and returns to staring at him. He stares back until he thinks out loud, "Am I okay? I'm not sure."

"Can I help you somehow? My name is Zella."

Gareth's eyes open so wide, the skin stretches across his forehead. "*Maybe I could just pretend I'm in one of Alysia's storybooks.*"

Then he remembers Mikita telling him to trust his intuition and in the way of things, so he says, "Hello, Zella. I'm Gareth. I'm not sure if you can help me, I'm on an exploratory."

"Nice to meet you, Gareth." Zella leans her head to the side. "Are you following the path on your journey?"

"Again, I'm not sure." Gareth shakes his head.

"How about we walk together and talk for a bit?"

"Okay, sure, why not?" Gareth catches up to where Zella is standing, and she walks alongside.

"Tell me, why are you on an exploratory?" asks Zella.

"To improve my creativity. I'm an architect," replies Gareth.

"An architect?"

Gareth smiles. "I create building designs."

"Oh, look around you, nature is a miraculous designer."

"I've been getting that lately."

"When you look around you with your architect eyes, what do you see?"

Gareth looks around and he takes many steps as he tries to put an answer into words. "I don't know. From a broad perspective, I see lots of symmetry but in the details, there is asymmetry."

"Yes, balance. Overall, there is a balance to all things. What else?"

"Complementary shapes and colors. The golden-yellow grass complements the green leaves."

"Yes, beauty. The grass complements the leaves as much as the leaves complement the grass. You have started to understand." Zella snorts through her nostrils. "There is beauty and balance in all of nature. That is the way of things."

Gareth continues walking and allows his mind to take in everything. "Yes, I suppose so."

"What happens after you design the buildings?"

Gareth smiles again. "Well, if the right people like them, we build them. We bring the designs to life."

Zella looks at Gareth. "You build them too?"

Gareth replies, "Yes, with other people. It's not something that can be accomplished alone."

Zella lifts her head and laughs. "Why didn't you say so?"

"Why didn't I say what?"

"You want to see the master builders. You need to travel south towards the large savanna."

"The master builders?"

"Yes, absolutely. We will head south now; I will escort you as far as I can."

Gareth looks at the ground and eyes the path. The reluctance to leave its clear direction grows. It takes a moment for him to remember he has the compass in his backpack.

Zella has already started off the trail and looks back over her shoulder. "Are you coming?"

"Just a minute," replies Gareth. He takes the compass out of the backpack and aligns it to find the south. The S on the compass points at Zella and he can't hold back a smile. Once he puts the compass safely back in the compartment, he takes out the opened water bottle. The water feels like silk smoothing out his rough throat. He holds up the empty bottle and says, "Thank you." Then he takes off for where Zella is waiting.

They walk along until they almost meet with the antelope herd. Zella looks at Gareth. "I'm going to call the herd over and tell them where we are headed. Don't be alarmed."

"Got it," replies Gareth.

Zella looks around and raises her nose to sniff the air before calling out, "Hey everyone. Come say hello to Gareth."

The herd comes directly over and surrounds Zella and Gareth.

"This is Gareth, he is on exploratory to the large savanna. I will escort him to the edge of the grasslands," says Zella.

Gareth can hear a variety of voices and phrases traveling on the breeze. They greet and welcome him until the talking fades.

One of the largest antelope approaches Zella and says in a deep voice, "Zella, you must be very cautious. The southern grasslands are cheetah territory."

Some of the herd echo their concern and say, "*Chee-tahh.*"

"I understand. Thank you." She nods her head more than once. "Gareth is on exploratory to see the master builders."

"Really? No one has traveled to see them in my lifetime. That is a special journey." The antelope lowers his head and takes a few small steps back before rejoining the herd.

Zella addresses the herd. "I will be back before sunset."

A high pitch voice calls out, "Good luck, Zella and Gareth." The herd turns and goes back to grazing and traveling.

Gareth stays with Zella, who watches the herd depart. She turns her head, and they begin walking south again.

"Are there really cheetahs?" asks Gareth.

"Why, of course, there are cheetahs. Many in the herd don't have experience with the cheetahs, so they stay away from where they hunt, but it will be okay. I will stay extra alert."

"Great, thank you. Can the cheetahs run as fast as the wind?"

"Yes, they are quick and can out pace some antelope on a sprint. But their sprint doesn't last as long as our stamina. Balance in all things, right?" She looks at Gareth and they both laugh.

"I suppose so." He says and they laugh some more.

The two of them hike on and occasionally pass patches of green grass with one or two trees. They take a break at one of the oases of green, and Gareth eats a few granola bars while Zella grazes. He opens another water bottle and uses the compass to orientate himself to a landmark in the south. He dislikes the thought but takes comfort in being prepared should he get separated from Zella. Gareth stands and pulls the straps of the backpack up his shoulders.

Zella walks over and says, "Are you ready?"

"Yes, shall we?" Gareth extends his arm to the south.

"We shall," says Zella, and they walk together.

Gareth enjoys the hike while he and Zella talk and have an occasional laugh. The sun has risen high in the sky, but they are making progress because ever so slowly, the grass is being replaced by more and more patches of trees. They halt their banter when Zella stops as if she bumped into an invisible wall.

"Shhhh," she says, and she lifts her nose to the air, sniffing in different directions. She looks around and sniffs the air again. She turns to look at Gareth. "There is a cheetah nearby." After scanning the surrounding area, she whispers, "Come, head to the patch of higher grass next to the incline."

Gareth follows Zella, trying to be as quiet as possible in his heavy hiking boots. He admires her graceful steps that don't make a sound as she moves through the grass. They crouch down and he sees a cheetah walking to a nearby patch of trees. "I see it," he whispers. His eyes stay on the thin cat with an elongated tail. Its body is covered with golden-yellow fur accented with dark spots and it slinks along with each step. "*It really is magnificent*," he thinks. As it comes closer to their view, he notices it walks with a limp in one of its hind legs and some of its fur looks ruffled.

"It's Citra. She's very old," says Zella. Citra approaches the largest tree in the patch. Zella raises her nose to the air and sniffs in different directions. She bows her head towards the ground. "She is dying," she says, and bravely looks at Citra.

"Really? Let's get out of here," whispers Gareth.

"No, we must stay out of respect. Would you rush off if she was giving birth? You don't have to watch, bow your head. She is about to enter a new phase, a new journey of her body and spirit. It is the way of things."

Citra lays down under the large tree and the side of her body rapidly rises and falls as she tries to catch her breath.

"She has returned to the tree she played under when she was a cub," says Zella.

Citra's breath slows, and as if she is taking deep breaths the side of her body raises higher than before and lowers more deeply.

Zella continues to tell Gareth about Citra. "In her life she has successfully raised more than half dozen cubs to adulthood. She will leave a void and be missed but that void will be filled by all that she has passed on to others, including her adult cheetahs."

The side of Citra's body raises and with a few twitches lowers into stillness.

Zella bows her head and mumbles a few words Gareth can't make out.

Gareth fights back a few tears that are stinging his eyes. "*So humbling*," he thinks and bows his head alongside Zella. When he looks up again, three other cheetahs surround Citra's body. They sit on their haunches in a ring facing her and raise their heads in the air while making high-pitched whimpers that transform into high-pitched chirps.

Zella looks at Gareth. "Now, we should get out of here. Be as quiet as you can. They are distracted but have keen hearing." Zella leads the way out of the tall grass and walks far away before turning completely to the south. They remain silent as each of them processes what they witnessed. Zella trots along until she snorts and slows her pace.

"Can I ask you a question?" says Gareth.

"Of course," replies Zella.

"When you said Citra was entering into a new phase of body and spirit, what did you mean?"

"Well, the same as her physical body will become a source of life for other living things as it returns to the soil, her spirit will return to the way of things. The spirit inside each life that sustains, the inner most part."

"So, in a way, you see dying as a continuation of life?"

"Yes, a continuation of life in different forms. A reason to experience loss and celebration. How spirit transforms, none of us really know until we go on that journey."

"You're saying Citra lives on in all those she touched during her life, in her continuation of the life force her body provides for nature and her innermost spirit returning to the way of things?"

"Absolutely." Zella turns to Gareth. "But the herd doesn't think about it so much, we just know that it *is*. That is the way of things." She snorts again and looks ahead.

They walk past another green oasis still heading south.

"Hey, can you show me how you walk through the tall grass without making a sound?" Gareth looks at Zella and laughs.

Zella laughs too and says, "I'm not so sure I'm that good of a teacher."

The patches of green grass and trees become denser, and once the trees become blended with the entire landscape, Zella stops. "We are near the edge of the grasslands. I can't escort you any further."

Gareth clears his throat. "I can't thank you enough for staying with me all this way."

"You are welcome. Head south and look for a large, tall structure made of earth. It will be a mound about three or four times your height." She pauses. "Good luck."

"Good luck to you as well. Have a safe journey back to the herd," replies Gareth. He watches Zella turn and begin walking north. A slight weight on his chest develops with her departure.

Discoveries

Gareth hikes south and pauses when he sees a large structure like Zella described, so he heads that direction. The breeze increases and he hears the trees rustle. His eyes scan the horizon, and he notices a hazy brown fog approaching. He picks up his pace, focused on his destination, hoping to escape an encounter with the ominous mass. After a few minutes, he glances to the side, and the mass is rolling on the ground like a cloud. The wind increases and bits of dust swirl around where he is walking. "*It's a dust storm. I better get a move on.*"

The dust storm rolls along and takes on a life where it seems to breathe as it grows higher. It travels closer and Gareth accepts he will have to face the storm, so he breaks into a jog. His mind calculates the direction of the approaching dust storm and wind with the location of the structure to determine the best spot to shelter. He keeps jogging and his respiration increases. In the hot afternoon temperature, sweat rolls down his forehead and the back of his neck. He draws close to the mound. "*Don't look back at the storm,*" he thinks.

Dust fills the air as the wind makes a strange, thunderous sound. The fine particles flying around sting Gareth's face and threaten to get into his eyes. He dives to the ground on the side of the mound. As quick as he can, he opens the backpack and pulls out the windbreaker. He slides it on, zips the zipper all the way up all the way up and is grateful to find it has a hood. Then he crunches in a fetal position on the ground next to the mound, pulls his shirt over his nose and mouth, and tucks the backpack next to his head. The wind surrounds him, and small swirling gusts propel dust through any small crack it can find. He pulls the backpack in tighter and closes his eyes.

While getting his labored breathing leveled out, Gareth remembers Citra lying under the tree and bits of the conversation with Zella. His chest aches, and his throat hurts. He starts to weep, and it increases until the tears create small pools in the sand. He weeps for the life he once had. He weeps for the void that losing Caitlin left in his world. He weeps for all the sacrifices it took to be a good single father. He weeps for all the times he couldn't go watch the basketball game with his friends.

Gareth gasps in a few desperate breaths, just as a gust of wind swirls around the back of the mound with such force it pushes his body against the structure, and dust penetrates his makeshift barrier. He is overtaken with a wave of lightheadedness, but this time it's a slow feeling of a half spin that destroys his equilibrium. After another gasp, his thinking shifts. He remembers the love that he carries for Caitlin, which he has to share with others. He thinks about how much of Caitlin carries on in Alysia. He feels the love he has for Alysia and how much she inspires him with her incredible imagination and how she invites him to engage in that world. Then, he remembers one of the things that got him through the funeral. It was that Caitlin's spirit was no longer stuck in her body that was suffering from illness and, as Zella would say, her spirit became free to transform and to return to the way of things. An incredible weight lifts from his entire insides and he releases a breath out of his mouth.

The wind dies down, and Gareth figures the gust must have been the storm making its way out of the area. Dust is still flying around, so he stays huddled for a few more minutes. His breath returns to normal, and to his amazement, he is refreshed, somehow invigorated. Sunlight returns, so he sits up. The dust and debris that collected in the creases of the windbreaker slip to the ground. With caution, he pulls off the hood and looks around. Everything seems calm. Warm from being inside the windbreaker, he slides it off and opens the backpack. He spies the half full water bottle in the bottom of the pack. With one swift movement, he opens it and gulps the remaining water. When the last drop is finished, he licks his lips and swallows. He packs everything neatly into the pack and leans it on the mound.

He stands and inspects the gigantic structure. As Zella said, it's at least three times his own height and made of brown dried earth, similar in color to the surrounding ground. He walks around to the other side, and it has an oval shape with bumps that look like cylinders embedded in the building material.

A few steps away, Gareth admires the workmanship. A voice travels into his ear that says, "Hello, I see you found our home or at least part of it."

He looks at his shoulder and sees a strange looking insect that has an enormous head with two mandibles protruding from each side of its mouth. It has a shiny golden-brown body shaped similar to an ant. With a frown, he flicks it off his shoulder with his fingers.

"Yaowww-wheee!" exclaims the insect.

Gareth follows the direction the insect went sailing and looks on the ground. "Sorry, my mistake. You startled me." He gets on his hands and knees, searching with his eyes. He sees a blade of grass move and the strange insect climbs onto a patch of bare ground.

"Whew! That was a wild ride," says the insect.

Gareth chuckles. "So sorry, are you okay?"

"Yes, I'm good. My name is Woodly."

"Hello Woodly, glad to meet you. I'm Gareth and I'm on an exploratory. I traveled to see your impressive structure."

"If you let me come closer, I can tell you more about our home."

"Okay. I promise I won't brush you away again." Gareth stretches his hand out and sets it on the ground. Woodly traverses Gareth's fingers and sits on his palm. Gareth holds Woodly at eye level.

"What you are seeing are the vents that allow air to flow in and out of our home. The termite colony lives underground. We have tunnels all the way to the water table where we gather the mud to build everything."

"Really?"

"Oh yes, inside we also farm the fungus we eat and in the most protected part the queen continually lays her eggs."

"How many are in your colony?" asks Gareth.

"I'm not sure, over a million," says Woodly.

"You're kidding! How do you all work together?"

"We all have our roles, some work on the structure, some tend to the fungus, some care for the eggs and the young. We don't think about it so much, we just do what we do."

"Again, that's impressive."

Woodly extends an invitation to Gareth. "Want to go inside?"

Gareth looks at his own body. "Sure, but I'm huge compared to you."

"I'll show you. Just put me on your shoulder."

Gareth places his hand level with his shoulder and tips it so Woodly can slide onto a safe spot.

Woodly raises his front legs and navigates the slide. "Whee!" he says then turns to face the same direction as Gareth before getting comfortable. "Now, have a seat and close your eyes."

"Okay, I suppose." Gareth moves so Woodly doesn't tumble down his shoulder, sits crossed-legged on the ground and closes his eyes.

"Follow me!" Woodly enters the mound through a small opening and Gareth follows with his mind's eye. "Here we are below ground, and this is the main nest. This is where most of the activity happens."

"There are a lot of members in your colony. They are all working like crazy!"

"Yes, I actually have a simple job today." Woodly chuckles. "Let's go down to the cellar." He heads down to a space below the main nest.

"Wow, it's much cooler down here." Gareth looks up and sees circles inside of circles that are layered in a funnel shape until they meet with the ground. At the bottom, the circular plates are jagged and coated with white residue.

"The circles are made of mud, and they absorb moisture from the colony above. When the moisture evaporates it cools the main nest," says Woodly.

"That's incredible!" says Gareth.

"There's more. See the half circle spaces around the edges of the cellar?"

Gareth inspects the area around the evaporating circles. "Yes, I see them."

"Those are openings that continue above ground. They make the bumps you see on the outside of the mound. Eventually, those openings are connected to a main opening that you might call a chimney in the center of the mound. Let's go look at that next." Woodly climbs back up and navigates around the nest to a main opening that stretches to the top of the mound. "See, the walls of the chimney are solid but the smaller openings that are around the outside are porous so air to flows through them."

"I see." Gareth looks all around while giving his head a scratch. He looks back at Woodly waiting for more information.

"When the sun warms the mound during the day, the hot air flows up the openings around the outside and this pulls air down the chimney."

"This is almost unbelievable," Gareth comments.

"Then during the night, the process is reversed when mound cools. The cool air flows down the openings and that pushes air up the main chimney. That's how we keep the air fresh and the temperature constant in our home."

"So basically, you're saying the entire colony lives underground in an ideal environment maintained through moisture evaporation and air flow created by temperature variation?"

"Different termites use other methods to maintain their colonies. But yes, that's how this one works. One could say that the structure can breathe air on its own."

Gareth nods his head. "This is beyond inspiring."

"Excellent. Let's go back outside again," says Woodly.

Gareth opens his eyes to see the termite mound and Woodly still sitting on his shoulder. "Thank you for showing me your home. That was really cool."

"You're welcome. As far as I know, it took many years to build. These days we spend most of our time maintaining everything."

Gareth looks at the sun's location and thinks about the time. It's low in the sky, and he slides his feet out in front of him. He looks at the sun again. "Oh no, I didn't realize it's so late. I don't know if I have time to get back before dark."

"Where is your home?" asks Woodly.

"I live in Krane, but I need to get to the other side of the forest."

"Don't worry. You can cut across and find the path where the grassland meets with the forest. It shouldn't take you too long and that's the safest route."

Gareth reflects on his day and replies, "That's a relief."

"Good. Why don't you lower me back to the ground? I should get home myself."

Gareth raises his hand to his shoulder. When Woodly is ready, he lowers him to the ground. He stands to retrieve the backpack and takes out the compass.

"By cut across, do you mean head northwest?" Gareth points in that direction.

"Yes, that way. You'll be fine."

"Thanks for everything, Woodly." Gareth puts the backpack on and keeps the compass in his hand.

"Thank you too, we haven't had a visitor for many generations," says Woodly with a wave.

Gareth waves back to Woodly, then begins the hike back to the forest. While walking along in silence, he realizes how little time he spends by himself. He looks at all the scenery. His sight wonders to where the green grass blends into the brown grass, to the trees that raise above everything else, and to the sun that moves across the sky. Completely in the moment, he doesn't think about the building proposal or other worries. "*Here is where I am,*" he thinks and chuckles to himself. The trees pass alongside him, and the landscape changes to where the yellow-golden grass takes over.

Once the knee-high grass crunches under his feet, anticipation of returning home rises. Although it will be another week before Alysia is home, he can't wait to see her. He wonders what kind of artwork or imaginary scenario she will have to share. He thinks about seeing Emma too and grins as he contemplates how he will keep from telling her about the details from the day.

His mind wanders to work and how being creative is so fulfilling. How satisfying it is to make ideas in his mind into ones that are expressed in plans and then turning those plans into objects. Objects that can be seen, touched, and experienced with others. His chest fills with warmness, confirming that being an architect is what he was meant to be doing. An enhanced centeredness grows inside him, and he returns to taking in everything around him, occasionally focusing on a single blade of grass.

In a child-like moment, he tries to walk through the grass with silence and grace like Zella. He laughs and when he refocuses in front of him, there is a break in the grass which looks like it could be the path. Over his shoulder is the forest, and he scans down the tree line to look for the opening. It takes a few more minutes of hiking until he sees where the break in the grass meets with an opening in the forest.

After reaching the mouth of the forest, Gareth looks to the sky and by the sun's position, he gages that he will make it back to Mikita's just before sunset. In the coolness of the forest, he takes one last break and puts the compass in the backpack. Then his steps quicken as he follows the trail, and he sees the forest from the opposite direction than in the morning. The trees are even more lush as the existing leaves have stretched out while a few continue to burst from the remaining buds. The smell of moist forest fills the air, which makes the experience a complete package. When the dirt trail meets with the wood plank path, he steadies his pace to enjoy the last of his exploratory. Once again there is an opening in the trees, and he knows it's not far to the deck.

Gareth reaches the deck and with three smooth steps he's up the stairs. He sees Mikita meditating on her mat and stops. The second mat is still sitting next to her, and he looks around for a moment, contemplating what to do next. He slides the backpack off his shoulders and places it by the screen door. Then he sits crossed-legged on the empty mat and decides to allow his mind to relax and absorb all the information from the day. He closes his eyes, and an intense scatter of thoughts and feelings almost overwhelm him.

Gareth recalls the feeling of having an enhanced center to use as a focus. The thoughts and emotions fade, allowing wisps of concepts to rise until animated clips like tiny movies develop. He sees the sketch of his building and then the solar panels transform into different shapes. Once that is complete, the vision of the building is three dimensional and it's sitting on the northwest site where it would be built. The materials used to build the outside transform next and then he sees the ventilation system inside the walls. He flies around the building and takes it in from every angle. After having this full view, his mind quiets. Excitement fills his stomach, and his chest is so warm it wants to burst. The urge to open his eyes is strong, but he takes special care to refocus on being centered and to feel connected with the deck, the ground below, and the world around him until coming fully out of the meditation.

Gareth opens his eyes, and the sun is meeting the horizon. He looks at Mikita and quietly says, "I'm back. You told me to let me know." He watches her, and she remains motionless for what seems like a long time. Finally, he sees her eyelashes raise, but she sits for a few moments looking at the forest.

She turns to him with a warm smile. "Gareth, you have returned. How are you doing? How was your exploratory?"

Gareth smiles back. "I'm good, I'm really good. The exploratory was beyond what I expected."

"Really?"

"Yes, it was so many things. When I returned and rested my mind, I saw what to do with the design for the building." He puts his head in his hands.

"Are you okay? Let me get you some water."

"You don't have to do that, I'm fine." Gareth says, but she has already disappeared into the house.

Mikita returns with two water bottles and hands one to Gareth. She situates on her mat, looks at him and says, "Let's sit quietly for a few minutes."

The sun sinks below the horizon and warm colors streak across the sky. "So, you said it was really good and you have ideas for your building proposal?"

Gareth looks at her. "Yes, and yes. It's just a lot of information to, you know, process."

"Yes, that happens. It may take some time to process everything, be patient with yourself."

"Got it." He looks around the deck. "Did you get the backpack? I wanted to be sure to give it back."

Mikita lifts the water bottle and takes a few sips. "Oh yes, I grabbed it when I went inside to get the water." She looks at him. "How are you feeling?"

"I feel good, really centered and content."

"Good. That's perfect." Mikita stands. "It's been a long day and you should get home for some rest."

Gareth stands. "This is strange. I'm not sure how to thank you except to say, thank you. I'm very grateful for everything."

Mikita smiles and nods. "You are welcome. I'm happy to be a guide and especially today, you did the work." A silence lingers until she says, "It would bring me peace to see you go ahead and return safely home."

Gareth bows his head. "Thank you for your time, Mikita." He turns and walks down the steps, continuing to his car. With no additional thought, he starts the car, drives to Main Street, and gets on the highway.

During the drive, he watches the last of the sunset colors fade and a few miles from home he realizes he's exhausted. He pulls into the driveway and puts the car in park, wishing he could transport himself into bed. But he makes his way out of the car, up the walk, and enters the house. Just after closing the door, he heads for the refrigerator and scans the contents. His shoulders pull in tight when he sees the plastic container that still has some of Emma's homemade pizza. Not stopping to sit down, he takes the first bite. While closing his eyes, he chews the pizza, thinking that it never tasted so delicious. He finishes all the pieces before finding his pajamas and taking a quick shower. After the shower, he gets into bed where he falls to sleep before tucking his favorite pillow under his head.

It's Scheduled

Gareth walks into his office and grins when he sees the mobile sculpture floating in the slight air currents. He puts his bag down and since he's been there so much, the office feels like a second home. The slew of papers scattered around are finally distilled down to an amount that's manageable. He shifts around what is left in the pile of sketches and printouts of the proposed building. A knock comes from the doorway.

"Oh man, you have been working non-stop since the weekend," says Lem.

"I know." Gareth gives his head a scratch. "I'm just trying to get organized for my second meeting with Henry today. After that I will come up for air."

Lem nods. "I picked-up the proposal from Suzanne." Lem hands a large envelope to Gareth.

"Thanks," He opens the envelope and slides the papers halfway out.

"It was good to get a chance to meet her and see the studio. She took the time to go over her proposal with me. She's pretty cool." Lem smiles.

"Yes, she's pretty cool," says Gareth.

"Anyway, everything looks good. She made sketches of three original ideas we can talk about later."

"I have time now if that works for you. Then maybe I can bribe you to help me figure out which of these to take to the meeting." Gareth looks at the pile of papers he was trying to organize.

"Sure," says Lem.

Gareth pulls the sketches out of the envelope and lays them on the desk.

Lem stands next to him. "Of course, Suzanne and I have thoughts about which one would be best."

Almost immediately one of the sketches stands out to Gareth. He looks at them a little longer and any of them would complement the shape of the space. He eliminates one by turning it over and looks at the remaining two, but there is no doubt about it, he likes the one with six layers. It reminds him of the shape of the honeycomb.

The sculpture has birds, flowers, and prisms like *Diamond Birds*, but also has semi-transparent fluffy clouds floating in the top layer. Then the weight at the bottom is a blue droplet shape, like a drop of water, perhaps rain falling from the clouds. He looks closer and the name she printed on the bottom is *From Sky to Forest*. He slides it in front of Lem. "This one."

Lem throws his head back and laughs. "You're still tearing it up!" Recomposing himself, he continues, "Yes, that one. Thankfully, Suzanne feels the same, so we're all on the same page."

Gareth goes to the other side of the office and pulls out the drawing of the atrium. He lays it on the desk and places *From Sky to Forest* in the bottom corner. "For the final presentation, I was thinking of making a poster board by taking this drawing of the atrium and adding some people enjoying the space with Suzanne's more detailed sketch of the mobile sculpture in the corner. It's a warmer way to convey the idea of a community space than a computer-generated print."

"That's great. I'll put it together and get the poster board made. It's been so long since I worked on a concept drawing." Lem offers.

"Are you sure?" asks Gareth.

"Yah, it will be fun."

With an expanded smile Gareth says, "Excellent. Let's move on to the outside of the building." He puts a few large papers from the pile onto the desk. "For the meeting today, I was thinking about taking a sketch and a couple of printouts. These are the ones I think are best." Gareth hears a brief swishing sound and looks at the doorway where he finds Asmee is standing. He jars Lem with his elbow.

"Hello Asmee. How are you today?" asks Lem.

"I'm spectacular." Her eyes roam the office. "Wow, there's a lot going on here and Gareth, you look, well, so casual today. I hope you're not working too hard."

"No, not at all. Thanks for asking," says Gareth.

"Oh, good. Everything just reminded me of my sister. She put a lot into her work but as a single mother it took its toll on her and eventually her children." She looks down and shakes her head. "Such a shame," she murmurs.

Gareth feels heat rise from his knees all the way into his shoulders. "Sorry to hear about that situation."

"Thank you. Sometimes we just don't see things when they are happening." Asmee pulls her suit jacket down. "Anyway, I just wanted to say hello and see if there was anything you needed but I guess you're fine." She smiles at Lem. "You guys have a good day," she says before walking away.

Lem returns to looking at the papers on the desk and mumbles something indistinguishable.

Gareth releases a breath to refocus. "Here is what I've gathered, a sketch of the outside, pared with a more detailed print out that includes specifics about the dimensions. Then a separate sheet with a diagram of the ventilation system."

"This is great." He looks everything over again. "But do you have a more detailed one about the ventilation system? One that includes more dimensions?"

Gareth looks at Lem and turns to the pile. He pulls out another large print. "Yes, I have this one."

Lem looks it over. "If it were me, I would go with this one. That way, if Henry asks questions or wants more information, it's all here. It's not too cluttered or anything."

"Got it. I see your point." Gareth leans with his hands on the desk while nodding his head a bunch of times. "I'll go with that one." He looks at Lem. "Thanks once again. Now, I still have time to review everything and get out for the lunch hour."

"You're welcome." Lem gathers the materials for the atrium poster board before walking out of the office.

Gareth leaves the building for lunch. In the city, he observes the people and lets go of worrying about how much time is passing. When he returns to his office, his mind is full of details to jot down before his meeting. He finishes that, and it's almost time to meet Henry, so he gathers his materials and walks to the private office area. As usual, Carol is working at her desk.

"Hello Carol. I'm a little early but I have a meeting with Mr. Kravin," says Gareth.

"Hi Gareth. He's been running behind today. Would you like to take a seat?"

"Sure, that gives me a chance to review everything."

After getting comfortable, Gareth inspects each plan he brought for the meeting and returns to his list of details. He looks at the time and it's almost fifteen minutes past the hour with no sign of Henry. Even when he strains his ears, he can't hear voices by the door signaling the current meeting is about to finish. At twenty minutes past the hour, he stands and takes a few steps closer to Carol's desk.

Carol looks up from a report she has been proof reading and makes eye contact with Gareth. "This isn't like Mr. Kravin. Let me check-in with him." She stands, walks over, and raps on Henry's office door with her knuckle.

Gareth can hear a muffled voice call out, and Carol opens the door. She talks back and forth with Henry before closing the door. Turning to Gareth, she says, "Mr. Kravin apologizes for the delay and asks, if at all possible, that you stay here. He'll be out in a few minutes."

"Yes, of course. I will wait," replies Gareth. He sits back in the chair and reorganizes his papers. He stares at the office door, then focuses on the door handle. Voices travel closer to the door until it opens. Asmee is the first to walk out, followed by Henry. Asmee looks at Gareth and grows an enormous smile. Gareth feels heat grow from his calves all the way up his body and as it creeps up his neck, he wonders if his skin is blushing.

"Gareth, come on over. Apologies to keep you waiting," says Henry.

"No problem," replies Gareth.

"Everyone huddle around." Henry motions so Gareth and Asmee stand next to him around Carol's desk. Carol looks at Henry and gives him her full attention.

"Does anyone happen to know where Lem is?" asks Henry.

Everyone looks at each other, but no one has an answer.

Henry continues. "Carol, when we finish, please hunt down Lem and if I'm busy, give him an update."

"Certainly," she says.

Henry looks around at everyone before continuing. "I heard from Nova. They will be here for our presentations this week Friday."

"Friday? Isn't that earlier than expected?" asks Carol.

"It is early, but you know Nirvaan. A great presentation in a time pinch is an excellent presentation." Henry looks at Asmee. "Asmee, you're generally set. I want you to work with Carol to get the details completed."

"Yes, that's great," says Asmee.

Henry turns to Gareth. "We have a few minutes to look at your designs and then I want you to work with Lem."

"Got it," says Gareth.

"Carol, get all preparations completed. Order drinks and snacks."

"Yes, consider it done," Carol says as she makes a note.

"When we meet with the folks from Nova, Asmee will present first, followed by Gareth. Everyone has worked hard and is doing excellent. Let's also remember this isn't a competition. We want to offer Nova different options and that's the best route for our firm."

All three of them nod and keep their focus on Henry.

"Great, just great. Gareth, let's see what you got." Henry turns and walks into his office.

Gareth follows Henry and takes the shortest route to the table, where he lays out the sketch with the plans for the outside building and plans for the ventilation system.

Henry grabs the plans for the outside of the building and examines the details. He rubs the stubble on his face. "I see you reconfigured the solar panels. Can that be done at a reasonable cost?"

"Yes, I've been diligent about costs and the plans are within budget."

"Everything went well with the city and power company?"

"Yes, they see it as a benefit to them as well. The engineer is making the calculations and I will check-in with her to make sure everything will be done on time."

"Great, just great." Henry looks at the plans a little longer. "I see you also changed the exterior building material to concrete. This is great, absolutely great." He moves to the other plans. "What's this?"

"It's a high efficiency ventilation system that also helps to maintain the temperature within the building."

"You're kidding. Has this been done before?" Henry smiles.

"I'm not kidding at all. Variations similar to this idea have been successful. The engineer is also looking at the specifics and hopefully, can give a range of the increased efficiency. If it's not worth it, I picked out a couple of standardized systems for them to review."

"Great, just great." Henry rubs his stubble again. "You have more than enough for the presentation and to leave them with a nice folder of materials. Focus on making sure the big picture is clear."

"Got it. Absolutely," replies Gareth.

"Again, apologies for how the timing went today. You are nearly set, and Lem is the perfect person to help see it across the finish line. Unfortunately, I have other obligations for the rest of the day."

"I understand, thank you." Gareth gathers up the papers and walks out of Henry's office.

Just as he is about to pass Carol's desk, she says, "Gareth, hold up a minute."

He stops and faces Carol. "Yes, I'm sorry, my mind is in overdrive."

"Of course. I just wanted to check what you will need for the final presentation."

Gareth thinks for a moment. "So far, I will need two or three large easels. I also need some folders so I can get them prepared."

Carol adds a note to her list. "I will gather the easels for the presentation. You can find boxes of folders in the copy room with the Kravin logo on the front. They're on the shelf opposite where we store paper."

"Perfect. Thank you so much. You are very good at what you do, and it's appreciated." Gareth gives her a small bow. He can feel Carol's eyes follow him as he exits the office area.

Once Gareth gets to his office, he reaches his desk in three long strides. He looks around and assesses the work he's accomplished and what still needs to be done. As he rustles through a stack of papers, looking for the engineer's contact information, Lem breaks his focus.

"Oh man, presentations this Friday. I just talked to Carol."

Gareth develops a wide smile. "You got it. There's a lot to get done, but I'm sort of glad it's scheduled." He waves Lem into his office. "I was thinking of breaking-up the presentation by the look of the building, how it's environmentally friendly, the sense of community it generates and end with mentioning the other interior spaces."

"You're tearing it up," says Lem.

"Along with the poster board of the atrium, I was thinking of including poster boards of the two other plans we picked for the meeting with Henry."

"Sounds like a great strategy. I'll take care of all the poster boards. I was going to have the atrium one made tomorrow."

"Thanks, that would be great." Gareth nods before spying Asmee outside the door. He looks past Lem and gives her eye contact.

"Hello, hope I'm not disturbing anything," says Asmee.

"Not at all, just getting ready for Friday," says Gareth.

"It's an interesting turn of events." Asmee puts a hand on the doorway and leans towards Lem. "Lem, I was wondering if you had time to help me out with a few things tomorrow afternoon." Tense energy fills the room as Asmee flashes him a smile.

Lem shifts his body in her direction. "I would like to help you but we're pretty busy here," he says.

"Oh," Asmee pulls a hand to her chest and stands straight.

Gareth twirls his silver pen around his fingers. "Besides, don't you have Carol to help you get ready?"

Asmee looks at Gareth. "Yes, I guess you're right." She manages to smile and at the same time narrow her eyes a tad. "Well, don't stay too late and enjoy your evening."

Gareth and Lem remain silent until her footsteps fade in the distance.

Lem walks over to Gareth and pats his shoulder. "I knew you were in there somewhere."

"Thanks." Gareth sighs with relief. "Let's get a plan together to complete a polished presentation in a day and a half."

"Hand me that notepad and a pen so I can make a list," says Lem.

Lem sits on the chair across the desk and the two of them work into the evening. After Lem leaves, Gareth starts organizing presentation slides and short animated clips from the modeling software for another couple of hours.

Nova Visit

Gareth stands outside the conference room with his poster boards. Inside Asmee is still giving her presentation to Nirvaan, Judi, and Robert from Nova. Carol comes around the corner pushing a cart with an urn of coffee and drinks followed by a caterer with a cart of small sandwiches and a variety of cookies. She directs the caterer about where to place the cart and they finish setting them like fine dining tables.

"That looks great," Gareth says to Carol.

"Grebee's is fantastic. We've used them quite a few times." Carol finishes her inspection of the carts and looks at Gareth. "I see you found the easels."

"Yes, thank you."

A burst of laughter and loud talking comes from the conference room.

"They must be wrapping up," says Carol.

Gareth's stomach tightens, and he looks down for a moment.

Carol steps over to Gareth and puts a comforting hand on his shoulder. "Just think of it like a normal, everyday meeting. Eventually these types of presentations will be that anyway, it might as well be today."

"Got it." Gareth nods.

The conference room bursts open, and Henry leads the group. Gareth notices everyone is smiling. Even Nirvaan appears relaxed and enjoying talking with Henry. "*This isn't helping*," he thinks.

Lem comes out last and gives him a grin before getting his fill of mini sandwiches onto a plate.

Gareth enters the conference room and gets the poster boards on display. Then he readies the presentation and flicks through each slide to make sure everything works properly. He eyes what's left on the table, and it looks like everyone is sitting in the same places as the initial meeting. He sets the completed folders on the table in front of their chairs.

Henry's voice travels from the next room as he says, "So, we stay on time, let's get what we want and get back to the conference room." He is the first to return, and he looks at Gareth. "Do you want to grab something to drink before we get started?"

"Yes, that's a good idea," Gareth says. After he grabs a bottle of water and takes a few steps back towards the doorway, he sees Asmee standing with one hand on her chair.

Henry leans over in her direction and puts his hand on the folder Gareth placed on the table. "Asmee, you can sit this one out. You've worked hard. Why don't you take a break, and we'll meet up later?" says Henry.

"Oh. Sure, of course," replies Asmee.

Gareth slows his steps as she gathers her papers from the table.

Asmee places her coffee and plate on top of the pile. Once she is just past the doorway, she sees Gareth and losses balance of the stack. The coffee cup teeters, and coffee threatens to splash over the rim.

"Let me help you," Gareth says as he sets down his drink.

"No thanks, I got it," Asmee replies. Without a glance in his direction, she heads down the hallway.

Gareth takes a moment to open his drink and swallow a few gulps. Then he closes his eyes and pulls in a deep, cleansing breath. He focuses on allowing all the tension in his stomach to flow out with the air as he exhales. After opening his eyes, he straightens his posture and walks into the conference room. As he heads to the front, Lem puts a hand on his arm. Gareth stops and leans over.

"Tear it up," whispers Lem.

Gareth nods and smiles at Lem while rounding to the front of the table. He scans the activity in the room and picks up the remote.

Nirvaan looks at him. "Gareth, great to see you again."

"It's good to see you too." Gareth relaxes and smiles. "How are the sandwiches? They look good."

"They're delicious. You should get yourself a couple," says Nirvaan.

Gareth puts his hand on his stomach. "I'm fine for now but I look forward to trying them later."

Sensing everyone is ready, Henry addresses the group. "Let's get started. I'm sure everyone remembers Gareth. He's going to present an exciting vision for the northwest site so without delay, I hand things over to him."

"Thanks, Henry." Gareth uses the remote to turn on the screen. His first slide is titled, "The Building," and has a list of bullet points. He walks over to the first poster board that depicts the outside of the building and starts at the bottom covering the two floors of parking, the retail and restaurant spaces at the base, and the configuration of the conjoined buildings before continuing his presentation. "Each roof top forms into a triangular spire that meets at the middle point. They are lined with solar panels. With the shape of the individual parts of the building, the spires are more diffuse than the traditional spires seen in the city. This echoes the shape of the mountain tops. The highest spire in the middle would be rimmed at the bottom with solar panels and the top would be all glass, similar to the highest peaks in Great Mountain that are covered with snow."

Gareth pauses and looks at everyone around the table. "The shapes also complement the city, along with the spires made of modern reflective solar panels and the building being made of a mixture of gray concrete and deeper gray trim. Yet, the contrast between the materials gives it an ultra-modern futuristic feel. The building takes on the shape of mountains and from other angles, the shape of a small city." He looks at the screen. "Let's take this in through a clip of modeling software that circles the building with a backdrop of the surrounding area." He starts the clip and remains silent as it plays.

Silence passes, and he continues to the next slide titled, "Environmentally Friendly" with another list of bullet points. He looks at the screen. "The first environmentally friendly aspect is the solar panels. According to our engineer's calculations, they would provide the building with enough power and on most sunny days, an excess of power." He explains about connecting with the city's power grid and the benefits, then looks at Henry, who gives him an affirming nod.

Gareth continues forward with the presentation, the words flowing without effort. "Included in the engineer's calculations for the amount of the power required is having electric car charging stations available in over sixty percent of the garage spots. We can imagine an environmentally conscious person being drawn to live or work in a building that provides this service."

Gareth takes a few swigs from his water bottle. "The last point is a ventilation system that works to moderate the temperature in the building and maintain high quality air. It's a biomimicry design adapted for a four-season environment."

He walks over to the second poster board of the ventilation system. "The building has exterior walls constructed of concrete. Then there is an air space between them and the interior walls. The interior walls are made of a porous material that function the same as traditional walls except they allow air in the wall space to interact with air in the interior spaces. Then there are air vents that run from the ground into the wall spaces and the wall spaces connect with additional vents on the roof top."

Again, he scans the table to observe each person's facial expression. "The vents are automated to open and close based on the outside and inside temperature. In the warmer months, the sun warms the outside of the building during the daytime hours, pulling the air upwards. In the cooler months this process is reversed when the building cools during the nighttime hours and the air is pulled downwards."

Gareth points at the arrows on the poster board to illustrate further. "Because the air in the wall space can interact with the air in the interior through the porous walls, the natural air flow in the wall space works similar to a ceiling fan. In the warm months the rising air in the wall space pulls air in the interior spaces upwards, keeping the cool air from settling near the floor. In the cooler months the falling air in the wall space pulls the air in the interior spaces downward keeping warm air from collecting near the ceilings."

Gareth slows for a moment to clear his throat. "So far, our engineer's estimate this will increase the efficiency of cooling and heating the building by fifteen to twenty-three percent. Let's take this in through a clip of modeling software that illustrates the process first for the warmer months followed by the reverse process for the cooler months." He starts the clip and remains silent as it plays.

After the clip is finished, Gareth advances to the next slide titled, "The Community." He walks over to the final poster board of the atrium. "The atrium sits under the glass portion of the middle spire." He covers access to the retail spaces and restaurants from the inside, and the mobile sculpture before adding more detail.

Then he says, "Leaders from the Great Mountains Park have also agreed in exchange for a budget friendly retail space, that they would provide and care for foliage in the atrium. The foliage would include plants and small trees from the area, bringing more of the Great Mountains into the building. They also will consider running tours of the Great Mountains Park directly from the building."

Let's look at a clip of the atrium from different angles. Gareth turns toward the screen and plays a brief clip. This time he narrates as it runs. "The atrium space can be used to further bring community together through a variety of events. Imagine, for example, small concerts such as string quartets or smooth jazz on evenings and weekends. The space could also be rented to the public for semiprivate gatherings and celebrations."

Gareth advances to the next slide titled, "The Interior Spaces." Walking back to stand next to the screen, he begins, "Here we are to the interior spaces. In the current plan, the luxury apartments would mainly be located on the northwest side of the building, with views of the Great Mountains. Then the office spaces would be on the southeast side with views of the city." He covers a few details about the luxury apartments and follows this with the convertible works stations. For a strong finish, he plays a clip of the hexagonal workstations and how they would convert into collaborative work areas.

He allows a moment to pass before turning to everyone sitting at the conference table. "So, this is an ultra-modern building that complements its surroundings. It's environmentally friendly to a great degree, creates a strong community environment and welcomes all those who enjoy the city and the Great Mountains. A building that reflects what Nova discovered are the needs of Rolling Hill."

Gareth's mind comes full stop as he observes everyone staring at him without much expression on their face. He meticulously scans everyone to see if he finds some reaction. Nirvaan's eyes are open wide, but his face looks frozen in place. Henry has a blank expression and is holding a mini sandwich in midair. But Lem is trying to hide the smile stretched across his face with his hand.

Gareth fights off panic and continues to close. "Inside the folders you will find technical specifics such as measurements, the engineer's calculations, and a budget. Does anyone have any questions?"

The table remains silent, so Gareth stares at Henry. Out of the corner of his eye he sees Lem run his hand over his mouth then plop his hands on the table before turning to look at Henry.

Henry puts the sandwich back on his plate and wipes his hands with a napkin. "Thank you, Gareth. That was beyond, well, that was great. If you don't mind, please excuse us to finish up a few things."

"No problem." Gareth looks at the group from Nova. "Thank you for the opportunity and your time," he says with a nod.

"No, no, thank you," says Nirvaan.

Gareth exits the conference room and closes the door behind him, not sure what to think. By the time he gets to his office, thoughts are skittering through his mind. He falls into his desk chair and sighs. "*Maybe it was too much, it was too creative, there was too much detail. What was it that George said? Oh yah, it was beyond. Beyond what?*" He looks around the office and spies the mobile sculpture. After watching its slow movements for a few minutes, he straightens the piles of papers on his desk. Lem's voice carries into his office.

"Oh man, I knew you were going to tear it up, but you left them downright speechless," Lem says then he throws his head back and releases a hearty laugh.

Gareth tosses him a look. "So, is that a good or bad thing?"

Lem looks at him and his expression shifts to being serious. "Hey, I really don't know what they are going to decide, but that doesn't matter. I've seen a lot of presentations and what you did today was excellent."

Gareth turns from Lem and goes back to messing with the array of papers. He looks at Lem. "Thanks. We'll see how things turn out."

Lem shakes his head side-to-side. "Don't worry about how it's going to go. Enjoy the moment. You deserve it."

Carol appears, and she navigates her head around Lem. "Mr. Kravin just let me know he would like everyone to gather outside his office in ten minutes."

Gareth looks at Carol. "Got it. Thank you, Carol."

Gareth and Lem discuss high points of the presentation then walk together to the private office area.

Lem walks in first and Carol greets him. "Hello Lem. How are you? I haven't talked to you since earlier this week."

"I'm fantastic. Bet you're glad today is over."

"Yes, I'm glad it's over. So much detail!" Carol laughs and waves her hands in the air.

Carol turns her attention to Gareth. "Hello, I heard a little buzz about your presentation today." She leans his direction and whispers, "Good for you."

Asmee arrives next and joins the group. "Hello everyone."

"Hi Asmee. Nice presentation today," says Lem.

"Thanks. I'm confident about everything," Asmee says with a sideways grin.

"So, what are we going to do next?" Lem jokes.

Light laughter spreads across the small group.

Henry emerges from his office and joins the gathering. "I see everyone is here." His smile escalates and his eyes have a slight shimmer. "Today was great, just great. I expect we'll hear from Nova in the next week or two." His eyes touch each person in the huddle. "It's my privilege to have such a great team. You have worked hard, and I want everyone to take a long weekend." He raises a finger in the air. "I don't want to see anyone in this office until Tuesday. Understood?"

Everyone agrees and shares words of gratitude with Henry for the extra day off.

Then Henry says, "Carol made plates with the leftovers from today and they're in the break room fridge. Take a plate or two, grab some drinks and get on home. Great job, thank you." He turns and walks into his office.

"I guess he's telling us it's time to go," says Lem and he dashes out of the office area.

Gareth looks at Asmee and Carol. "Have a great weekend. I'm going to follow that lead."

Gareth heads to his office and remembers Alysia will be back at home when he arrives. He walks with longer strides. It takes no time at all for him to stop by the break room to pick up a plate and some drinks. He's glad he didn't skip it because he could tell Carol put the plates together with care. With Alysia and Emma in mind, he takes a plate of appealing cookies and a few drinks. In another flash, he gets to his office and packs his bag.

❋❋❋

Just before reaching the highway exit to Krane, Gareth decides to pick up dinner. Then they can have the cookies from the office for dessert. It will be a nice way to thank Emma and he imagines everyone sharing stories about their week. He pulls into Sunset Restaurant, where he orders a large salad to go along with their infamous family baked chicken dinner. His knee bops up and down while waiting for them to prepare the order.

When he pulls into the drive at the house, Gareth wonders how he is going to carry everything in one trip. He stuffs the should bag full then flings the strap over his head before creating a neat stack of the food containers. Once he reaches the house, he manages to open the door and get past the entry way.

Alysia appears from the hallway with her arms full of stuffed animals. When she sees him, she drops them on the floor. "Daddy!" She bats a few of the stuffed animals with her feet as she runs to him and grabs his legs.

Unable to bend over, Gareth says, "Hold on… I didn't think about this part. Let me put this stuff down so I can give you a big hug." He waddles to the kitchen with Alysia holding on to the bottom of his suit jacket, already prattling on about her week.

Emma emerges from the kitchen. "Oh my, it looks like you have enough food for the neighborhood." She meets Gareth and takes the containers off the top of the stack.

All three of them reach the kitchen, and Gareth puts the remaining containers on the table. Alysia is still at his side. He leans over and gives her a squishy hug. "I missed you so much." The hug ends, and he touches her nose with his finger. "Daddy had a very adventurous week."

"Really Daddy? Was it like one of my story books?"

Gareth raises his eyes to the ceiling as he remembers back to his exploratory, then leans close to Alysia. "Yes, it kind of was like those adventures."

"Wow," says Alysia.

"Wow is right. What were you doing with all your stuffed animals?" Gareth motions with his chin to the scattered pile on the floor.

"Oh, I missed them too, so I was bringing them out to sit on the couch."

"I see. Well, get them comfy on the couch so we can all watch a movie together."

"I like the sound of that." Alysia runs back to pick up the stuffed animals.

Emma works on setting the table. "Welcome home stranger."

"Hello Emma. So good to see you." Gareth smiles. "How did everything go?"

"You know I'm dying to hear how everything went for you, but I guess I'll start. Everything went really well, pretty much as we figured. Alysia was at the Recreation Center a lot and made friends with some children that live on my street. We also had a fantastic time. We made some crafts, I'm sure you'll see them all. Then we planted seeds, but those are still at my place to grow." Emma turns to look into the living room. "She did fine, but I think she got homesick the last couple of days and wasn't sleeping well because she's been a little cranky."

"Got it. That makes sense. I will give her my undivided attention and let her fall asleep with her stuffed animal herd on the couch, even if it's early." Gareth slides into a kitchen chair. "Early bed would be fine by me. I feel good right now, but I should be exhausted."

"So, what happened? How did your week turn out?" asks Emma.

"Let's see. I did the session with Mikita. It was super helpful, but she was right. It wore me out. I recuperated after that and kept working on the presentation. When I was supposed to meet with my boss for a second time, we found out the investment company was coming early to hear the presentations."

Emma puts a hand on her hip. "No way, really?"

"Yes, absolutely. I gave the presentation today."

Emma closes her eyes and shakes her head back and forth before saying, "How was it? I'm sure you were magnificent."

"It was strange." Gareth gives his head a scratch. "The folks from Nova, their reaction wasn't what I expected."

"How so?" asks Emma.

"Afterward, they were silent. They didn't say a word."

"Really? You took them by surprise." Emma smiles.

"I guess. Lem said the presentation was excellent."

"Lem's been in the business a long time. Right? You can trust his judgement." Emma's smile widens.

"Yes, but that doesn't tell me if they are interested in my building. Anyway, I'm glad it's done. It was a lot of work and it turned out to be a good thing Alysia was with you this past week. Thank you so much. You're staying for dinner, aren't you?"

"Of course, it was thoughtful of you to bring such a feast." Emma looks at Gareth, and her smile transforms into a mischievous grin.

"What?" asks Gareth.

"Nothing, I was just thinking about everything, and I think you're going to be surprised." While keeping her eyes on Gareth, she turns her head to the living room. "Alysia, how are you doing? Are you ready to come to dinner?"

The Final Act

Gareth enjoys a restful weekend that consists of playing with Alysia, hearing all about her week and getting their household organized. When he gets back to work, he's content to be on a normal schedule and so is Alysia. She even seems eager to get to school in the mornings. Just like at home, he works to get his office back in order so he can slow down before the next thing comes along. At the end of the week, he gets off the elevator after lunch and bumps into Henry.

"Hello, Gareth." Henry connects with his eyes. "You're going to be at the monthly office meeting this afternoon, right?"

"Absolutely. Same as always," replies Gareth.

"Great, just great. See you then." The elevator dings and the doors open. "I have a meeting in the city, but I'll be back." Henry steps into the elevator and the doors close.

Gareth heads to his office and takes his time getting settled at his desk. In his chair, he looks around and most everything is organized and clean. Spying the balsa wood model that he used to convert his ideas brings on a nostalgic grin. He doesn't have the heart to get rid of it yet to create space for playing with new ideas. His eyes roam to the corner of the room where the poster boards were sitting, but they have disappeared. Then he slides a sample architectural journal from the small pile of mail Carol left on his desk and begins flipping through the pages. A couple of articles grab his attention, and he gets absorbed in the information.

"Oh man, you never quit." Lem leans on the doorframe.

Gareth sits straight. "Hey Lem. It's nothing, just one of the sample journals we get all the time. I'm not starting anything new yet, if that's what you mean." Gareth chuckles. He looks over to the empty space in the corner of the room. "Did you pick up the poster boards?"

"Um, yah. You seemed determined to get your office all neat and tidy again," replies Lem.

Gareth gives him a lighthearted stare, followed by a grin. "Thanks, I guess."

"No problem. We should get going to the office meeting."

"Yes, it's time." Gareth stands and stretches before running his fingers through his hair.

As they walk down the hall together, Gareth straitens his tie and makes sure he has his pen. "Were we supposed to prepare anything for this meeting? With everything going on, I forgot all about it."

"I don't think anyone expects us to be focused on daily office stuff yet," says Lem.

They come around the corner and Henry is standing with Carol by the conference room door.

"Hello, are we ready?" asks Lem.

"Yes, we are just waiting for Asmee. Here she comes," says Henry.

Henry grabs the door handle to the conference room and stops. "Once again, I just wanted to thank everyone for the hard work." He allows an elongated silence to pass. "And you, Gareth," he says in a tone reminiscent of an angry parent and he points at Gareth with his free hand.

Gareth leans away from Henry. He feels everyone in the group staring at him and redness creeping up his neck.

Henry turns the handle and starts to open the door. "Well, you, I just wanted to congratulate you!" He flings the door open. "You did it. Nova accepted your proposal. You're going to build your building." He walks into the conference room with a wild laugh.

Gareth's mouth hangs open as he follows Henry into the room. Nirvaan and Judi are standing on the other side of the table and his poster boards are displayed where they were for the presentation. He leans over and lets out a breath. Once recovered, he looks at Henry with a toothy smile and red cheeks. "You really had me going there."

"Congratulations," says Henry.

"You've got to be kidding," Gareth walks further down the table. Nirvaan leans across the table and shakes Gareth's hand with emphasis. Judi follows Nirvaan's lead but presents Gareth with a more delicate touch. The room fills with chatter and laughter.

Carol and Lem come to Gareth's side.

"Congratulations, Gareth. I'm thrilled for you," Carol gives his shoulder a quick squeeze.

"I told you to tear it up, but I had no idea you would steal the words from their mouths," Lem says as he shakes Gareth's hand.

Gareth leans over again, this time overwhelmed by emotion. He hangs on to Lem's handshake until he stands upright again. "I couldn't have done it without your help," he chokes.

"Oh man, this is going to be great." Lem clasps Gareth's shoulder.

On the other end of the table, Asmee remains standing next to her normal chair. The color drains from her face and her expression goes blank while her lips curve downward. She looks like a gray statue, devoid of motion until she melts into her chair without a word.

The room quiets and Nirvaan walks to the presentation area. Everyone's eyes follow him, and he clears his throat to gain more attention. "Hello Kravin Team," he says and waits until the group is in listening mode. He looks over to Judi. "We wanted to congratulate Gareth in person, but Judi and I can't stay." Nirvaan looks down in thought before saying, "Here we are in a moment of celebration and a new endeavor on the horizon. When we saw Gareth's presentation, it's true, it left us speechless." Nirvaan bows towards Gareth.

Gareth bows in return and murmurs, "Thank you for the great compliment."

"It was as if he crawled into our minds and pulled out the building we had in our imaginations. The building we would design if we could design it ourselves." Nirvaan finishes with a laugh and soft laughter spreads across the room.

"This is an incredible accomplishment no doubt, yet serious work is about to come. We look forward to establishing a rapport with your team and creating the building that will be Nova's largest accomplishment to date. There will be no hesitation, we want to break ground this upcoming season." Nirvaan allows a wave of silence to pass through the room. "In fact, our associate Robert, also wanted to be here today, but he's working on securing the northwest site as we speak."

Everyone spontaneously claps and Nirvaan joins with a few claps of his own.

"So, please enjoy the moment and celebration as a team. Judi and I kindly excuse ourselves. We will see more than enough of each other very soon," says Nirvaan.

The sound of clapping flows through the air as Nirvaan and Judi slowly leave the room, shaking hands with Henry before they leave.

Gareth and Lem get settled in their normal chairs and switch their attention to Henry.

"Nirvaan was more elegant in his expression than I could manage," says Henry. He looks at everyone around the table. "Now is the time to celebrate and come together as a team. In looking to the future, like Nova this will be one of Kravin's largest accomplishments to date." He turns to Carol, who is sitting next to him. "Nirvaan was very serious in that they are not hesitating. Some wheels are already in motion, and they have been working with Carol to start a meeting schedule. So, please embrace this happy time and let it invigorate you." He raises his hand. "That's all I have to say for the moment. Stay and enjoy yourselves, I also must leave." He makes a smooth exit out of the conference room as everyone claps.

Once Henry leaves, Carol walks over to where Gareth is sitting. Gareth and Lem are engaged in lively conversation, so she pauses before saying, "Pardon me, but I have a message for Gareth from Emma."

Gareth's head pivots towards Carol, and his smile drops. He accepts the piece of paper Carol hands him.

"Emma told me to emphasize to you that everything is just fine. She just has a few things to do and asks that you pick Alysia up at her house today," says Carol to articulate what is in the handwritten message.

The smile returns to Gareth's face, and he nods. "Thanks Carol. Got it. Absolutely, I will pick Alysia up at Emma's house." He looks at the paper and draws into himself. "Emma had Alysia for an entire week. I'm sure it's taken time away from her normal activities," he says out loud.

Lem jumps out of his chair. "That reminds me, I have to get going. There's somewhere I need to be soon. See you later." He gathers the poster boards and dashes out of the room.

Gareth looks at Carol. "I guess the meeting is over."

"I guess so," Carol says, and she folds up the empty easels.

"Let me lend you a hand." Gareth rises and folds up the easel closest to him, and they walk out of the room together.

Carol turns off the lights before closing the door.

"I think I'm still in shock. Did that all just happen?" Gareth halfway jokes.

"Indeed, it did." Carol takes the third easel from Gareth. "Go on now, pick up your daughter and have a wonderful evening."

Gareth heads to his office. Just like every other day, he packs his bag, looks around to survey the landscape and leaves.

The drive from Rolling Hill, past Krane and onto Tree Side Village takes over half an hour. This gives his mind plenty of time to rotate from replaying every moment since lunchtime to blissful silence encased in an intense joy. He can't imagine telling Emma and explaining to Alysia about what has happened. He pulls onto Emma's street and as he nears the house, he notices a sign on the tree lawn. The car takes him closer, and he says out loud to himself, "Oh no, she didn't." Almost to the driveway, he reads the sign, "Congratulations Gareth!" He pulls in the drive littered with a few extra cars he doesn't recognize and says, "Oh yes, she did." Before stepping out of his car, he embraces that other people want to share this moment with him.

He walks up to the door and knocks a few times. Then he opens the door just enough to peek inside. "Emma?"

Emma approaches the door and pulls it wide open. "Hey Gareth! We wanted to surprise you."

Gareth steps in the doorway to find familiar faces filling the room, and Alysia comes running in his direction. He leans over and opens his arms to receive her hug.

"Daddy! Aunt Emma said you did good."

He wraps Alysia up in his embrace. "I sure did, sweetheart. I sure did." He lets her go and meets her eyes.

"Come see, everyone is here for you."

"All right." He takes Alysia's hand and stands so he can see all the guests in Emma's house.

Emma raises her glass. "We congratulate Gareth in his accomplishment, and we are excited to share in the joy and hope it brings."

The group raises their glasses and utter words of praise before taking a drink.

Gareth responds, "I can't thank everyone enough. Just the same as the balance found in all things, if it wasn't for all of you, this moment wouldn't have happened."

Everyone claps, which increases the warmth growing in Gareth's cheeks. He looks at Alysia and they walk farther into the house. A few people surround them and convey their immediate congratulations.

Alysia tugs at his hand. "Can I go play now?"

He inspects the group of children playing in the next room. "Sure, but let me know if you need anything. Okay?"

"Okay." Alysia runs off to the other room, escaping the crowd of tall adults.

Emma approaches Gareth and nudges her way close to him. "I'm sure you would like something to eat or drink. Come, this way." Emma guides him to the dining room.

"Thanks Emma. I really appreciate all of this, it's just a little overwhelming."

"I understand. Everyone will break up into groups now. Would you like something to drink?" she asks.

"Sure, a bottle of lemon seltzer would be perfect."

She grabs a bottle from the cooler and hands it to Gareth.

He opens the bottle and takes a few drinks. As he lowers the drink from his mouth, he sees Mikita across the room. "Mikita is here," he says, and looks at Emma.

"Of course, I invited her." Emma smiles and turns in Mikita's direction.

"I should talk to her and thank her again."

"That sounds like a good idea." Emma inspects the table, picking up stray plates and looking for any platters that could use replenishment.

Gareth walks to where Mikita is standing, and she turns his direction. Without thinking, words come from his mouth. "Mikita, how comforting it is to see you again." To him, the room spins around them, and the rest of the world disappears. He doesn't even hear the intermingled conversations that float throughout the house.

Mikita reaches out with a warm smile. "Gareth, you succeeded in what you wanted to accomplish. How wonderful."

"Yes, thank you."

"And look at all those who gathered here this evening." She scans the room.

He looks at her hands and resists the urge to grab both of them so he can pull them close to his chest. "Yes, but I really wanted to thank you. If it wasn't for the sessions, if it wasn't for the exploratory, I wouldn't have been successful."

Mikita bows to him. "You are most welcome. As I mentioned before, I'm happy to be a guide but you did the work." She looks into his eyes. "Follow me."

Gareth watches as she navigates around people with grace to reach the adjoining sunroom. He follows her path, not sure what to expect. As he looks around the doorway, he sees the poster boards from work displayed. Ellen and Suzanne are standing next to the one depicting the atrium with the mobile sculpture while Thomas is taking pictures. Gareth stops and observes the activity until Ellen sees him.

"Gareth, we are so excited! Congratulations and what an accomplishment," Ellen says while walking over to him.

"Ellen, I'm glad you and Thomas are here. This is an accomplishment for everyone. Who would have thought?" Gareth slides his hand across Ellen's shoulder as he walks closer to the poster boards where Suzanne is standing.

"Suzanne, congratulations! Your proposal and sketches were an intricate part of how things turned out. Just as you see on the poster boards," says Gareth.

"Sure, sure. Thanks," Suzanne says as she breaks a broad smile. "I see you went with *From Sky to Forest.* That's the one Lem, and I discussed."

"Oh yes. Each sketch was great, but from what I understand all of us favored that one. Agreement is an excellent was to start a project."

"You got that right," says Suzanne.

Lem's voice reverberates from across the room. "Mikita? Is that you?"

"Hello Lem. It's good to see you, it's been a while," replies Mikita.

Gareth and Suzanne turn towards Lem, who is walking into the room with a fresh drink in hand.

Lem circles Mikita. "You look great! You're so grown up that I almost didn't recognize you."

Mikita nods while saying, "I could say the same about you."

"How's your father? I haven't seen him for years. He really helped me, you know, find my way."

"He's good. Retired from leading weekly services and he enjoys having the time to refine his writings."

"And you have taken the lead on the services?" asks Lem.

"Yes, it seems that I have."

"That's great." Lem pauses and pulls his eyebrows closer together. "What are you doing here?"

"Emma invited me, and I know Gareth from services." Mikita looks over to Gareth with a slight blush rising in her cheeks.

"Wait, a minute." Lem slows his animation as he looks from Mikita over to Gareth. "Has Gareth taking part in spiritual practices been a recent thing? Have you been coaching him?"

"Why don't you ask him?" Mikita replies.

"Gareth how is it you know, Mikita?" calls out Lem.

Gareth excuses himself from conversing with Suzanne to join Lem and Mikita. "Hey Lem. So, you're how Emma knew about everything and got this party together. I forgot you grew-up in Tree Side."

Lem shrugs. "Guilty as charged. After you talked to her, Emma just kind of knew and sought me out. She's good at working things out in the background."

"Yes, she sure is." Gareth chuckles.

Lem asks again, "How do you know Mikita?"

Gareth looks at Mikita and clears his throat. "Um, for years I put my spiritual practice skills to the side and Mikita worked with me to get back into everything."

"Has this been recently?" Lem moves his eyes from Mikita to Gareth, looking for a clue.

"Yes, I guess so," replies Gareth.

Lem throws his head back and laughs. Still laughing, he changes direction and leans forward until he almost spills his drink. "I should have known!" He looks at Mikita. "It was like watching someone coming back to life. All these things that I knew were inside of this guy came out in the best possible way."

Mikita laughs with Lem. "Yes, that happens."

Gareth feels the warmth return to his cheeks. "All right, you two." He looks over his shoulder and sees a few people with Emma. It looks like they are getting ready to leave and he considers how everyone was already there when he arrived.

Lem and Mikita continue talking but shift the topic to Ellen's gallery.

"Sorry but I'm going to make sure I have time to talk to everyone before they leave," says Gareth.

"Sure, of course," replies Mikita.

Gareth methodically seeks anyone he hasn't been able to connect with by moving from cluster-to-cluster of people. He enjoys each conversation and expresses gratitude as a trickle of guests bid their farewells. Eventually the house is empty, and his eyes feel heavy. He helps Emma with the last of the cleanup and gives her a special goodbye embrace. Alysia can barely stay awake as they get into the car, while he hopes that once they get home, he will be able to sleep at all.

MIKITA

City Visit

After the Spiritual Practitioners Conference in Rolling Hill, Mikita pulls the slip of paper Emma gave her from her pocket, and reads the address. Then she walks along and finds herself in front of a skyscraper that is so tall that she has to lean back to see the top. "*I'm here now, I might as well go through with it*," she thinks and opens the door to enter what she thought would be a lobby but sees the elevators. She pushes the button and rides the elevator up to the tenth floor. The doors open and stepping into the hall she finds Kravin Architecture.

Mikita sees an office area where there is a woman working at her desk and approaches the woman. "Excuse me, I was wondering if you could tell me where I could find Gareth's office?"

"Hello, I'm Carol. I'd be happy to help you. Do you have an appointment with Gareth?"

"Well, maybe, I don't know if Emma told him I might stop by today."

Carol produces a soft smile. "Let's check if he's in." She stands from her chair and leads Mikita out of the private area.

They walk down the hall and Carol says, "Here we are." She wraps her knuckles on the door. After a brief pause, she steps into the office while Mikita waits in the hall. Carol quickly emerges back into the hallway. "You can go on in. Have a delightful afternoon."

"Thank you for showing me the way," Mikita says with a minute quiver in her voice. She watches Carol get part way down the hall before poking her head past the doorway.

Gareth is already on his way over. "Mikita, how good to see you. Please, come in. Emma mentioned it to me, but I can't believe you stopped by." He walks to his desk and raises a hand to the other chairs. "Have a seat, make yourself comfortable."

"I'm glad Emma told you; I wouldn't want to show up unannounced."

"Emma is very good at working things out." Gareth smiles.

"Yes, she is good at that." Mikita sits in a chair without sliding back into the seat. "I just thought I would come by and see how you were doing."

Gareth leans back in his chair. "Oh, I'm great. It's been like a whirlwind." He sits upright and leans forward on the desk. "I'm sorry I haven't been back to Tree Side for so long. What has it been? Almost a year now? I didn't expect to get the project and to be so busy."

"That's completely understandable." Mikita notices Gareth has a beaming smile, his completion is rosy, and the top buttons of his shirt are left undone.

"So, how about you? How are you doing?" he asks.

"I've been good. I've been in town for a Spiritual Practitioner's Conference earlier this week."

"Really? How did that go?"

"It was pretty fast-paced. I met a bunch of people and attended some great workshops. A group of us spent a night in Great Mountains Park. It's exquisite and takes you away from everything."

"Yes, it's an experience being in the mountains." Gareth nods. "Hey, I was just about to go visit the site. Would you like to see what we have completed?"

"Sure, why not? It sounds like an adventure."

"I don't know about an adventure, but they installed the mobile sculpture today. Hopefully it went well." Gareth gives his head a scratch before saying, "We can walk if that works for you."

"Yes, I would enjoy walking."

"Great." Gareth stands and allows her to walk out of the office first. They make their way down the elevator and out onto the city street. "Let's cross at this intersection. Then we'll just head down the sidewalk."

"Rolling Hill has really grown since the last time I was here." Mikita looks at all the buildings.

"It really has. What I notice too, is there's much more activity. People out enjoying the city."

"Yes, yet it still has the characteristics of a transient city. People are very talkative. They like giving directions and advice about the best places to visit," says Mikita.

"I hadn't thought about it, but I guess you're right. It's different from Krane or Tree Side."

The two of them make eye contact and chuckle. They walk along at a good clip for a couple more blocks in silence.

"We'll be able to see it soon. I always feel astonished when I first look at it," says Gareth.

The building comes into view, and Mikita halts her steps. "Oh my, Gareth, it's incredible. I got a glimpse of it on our way out of the Great Mountains, but I really didn't process."

"Come on, there's more. The main structure is completed, and the interior is in progress." Gareth keeps walking.

Mikita takes a few quick steps to catch up with him and remains silent as she absorbs the entire building. They reach the edge of the construction site and follow the fencing to a small trailer.

"We'll go in here and I'll sign in. Hopefully, I don't get sidetracked by things that need to be addressed right away," says Gareth.

They walk into the trailer and Mikita watches as many of the workers inside greet Gareth. "I'm here to check out the sculpture insulation," he says.

One man says, "Oh yah, you just missed Lem and Suzanne. Everything went well, it looks good." He whistles with his lips.

"That's what I like to hear," says Gareth.

A woman approaches Gareth with a clipboard holding some papers. "I need you to sign this." She leans closer to him, using a pen as a pointer while going through the items in the document.

"Thanks, all right." Gareth takes the pen and signs the document. Then he looks around. "Everyone, this is Mikita. She's my guest and a friend of the artist."

A few people wave and say, "Hi Mikita."

Mikita gives them a nod and shy wave back.

Gareth walks up close to her. "You'll have to wear a hard hat. I think this one is adjusted so it will fit okay. Give it a try."

Mikita takes the hard hat, inspects it, and places it on her head. "I knew this was going to be an adventure." She moves the hat around. "Yes, it feels okay."

"Good." Gareth puts on a hat that has his name on the back.

The same man who spoke previously stops them before they leave. "You might want to take a flashlight with you, the custom lighting still isn't installed in the walkway."

"What? Why not?" asks Gareth.

"It just arrived today."

"Fine, I will follow up on the lighting first thing on Monday. Today I'm here about the installation," Gareth grabs a flashlight and guides Mikita out of the trailer.

"Sorry about all that, it goes with the territory," Gareth mumbles.

"It's fine. I thought it was pretty interesting." Mikita grins.

Gareth places a hand on Mikita's lower back. "Let's go this way, there's a path. Of course, one day this will all be landscaped."

They walk across the field of dirt, closer to the building. "Finally, the front door." Gareth opens the door where they step into a dimly lit area. He turns on the flashlight and shines it around. "This will be a walkway with multi-color lighting. It will pull people into the building and make them feel like they entered a different world."

"That's wonderful. Is that light from the atrium at the end?"

"You got it." Gareth shines the flashlight down the walkway.

Mikita anticipates the sun filled atrium as they approach. Once they reach the area, she looks in all directions. "Oh my, this is beyond impressive."

Gareth walks farther into the atrium and cranes his head upward. "There it is, *From Sky to Forest.* And it looks even better than I expected. That's fantastic." He keeps walking until he's directly under the mobile. "The prisms are just right."

Mikita walks over and stands next to Gareth. She looks upwards at the mobile and around the huge atrium. "At this point, I'm at a loss for words." She takes a few steps away from him while continuing to inspect the mobile. Bits of colored light from the prisms float around the space giving it a magical feel. She turns to face him. "So, let's get this straight. You purchased a mobile sculpture from Ellen's gallery. Ellen gave you the artist's card, so you tracked her down and she contributed to your building proposal. Now, her artwork will be enjoyed by everyone that enters this atrium?"

"Yes, absolutely. This space is for the entire community, not just the people who will live and work here but also for everyone who enjoys the retail spaces or just pass through for that matter." Gareth scans all the entrance ways. "This space will also have events and be available for celebrations."

"And you created the vision for this wonderful building that a countless number of people will enjoy whether they live or work here, visit here or even see it from the outside?"

"Well, yes, absolutely."

Mikita looks down and slides one of her feet back. She looks at Gareth again. "The interconnection of community is amazing." She radiates a warm smile.

Mikita feels the intensity of Gareth's stare before he says, "Mikita, there's something else I want to tell you."

"Oh, what's that?"

"The one-on-one sessions with you changed my life in many ways but how everything worked out is I started attending spiritual practices in Krane with Jayden again."

"I see." Mikita crosses her arms. "Of course, if that's for the best. I got to meet Jayden this week, and he's very knowledgeable."

Gareth takes a small step to the side and shifts back to facing Mikita. "Yes, perhaps it's for the best because I was also thinking that I would like our relationship to change from what it has been in the past."

"Do you mean as us becoming friends?"

"Not exactly. I was wondering if you would let me take you to dinner tonight."

"Oh." She pauses. "On a date?"

Gareth clears his throat. "Yes, on an official date."

Mikita returns to looking at the mobile. Then she walks over to stand next to Gareth. She looks at him and says, "Yes, I would like that very much."

"That's great." Gareth moves his eyes to the mobile again.

After a few minutes Mikita says, "Are you ready to go? Is there anything else you need to do here?"

"No, I accomplished everything I needed," Gareth says with a grin. He extends his hand in Mikita's direction.

Mikita places her hand into his and they wrap their fingers around each other's grasp. They keep holding hands as they walk out of the building that's still under construction.

About the Author

Laura is the author of fiction stories that say something through a twist on reality. Common themes behind the words include raising consciousness, facilitating high vibrational energy, and supporting the soul's journey. Academically, she has a master's degree in Philosophy and served as Adjunct Faculty in the Humanities. When she isn't reading and writing, she spends time connecting with others, enjoying nature, and watching all kinds of documentaries. To subscribe to *Laura's Latest* newsletter or contact her visit: www.lauraclementzauthor.com

One Final Note

Thank you for reading, *Exploratory Tales*. Reviews mean a lot to authors and other readers. If you enjoyed the book, please consider taking a moment to leave a short review at Amazon.com and if you are a member of the community, at Goodreads.com.

www.ingramcontent.com/pod-product-compliance
Lightning Source LLC
La Vergne TN
LVHW050620100826
845148LV00011B/1661

* 9 7 8 1 7 3 4 0 4 9 7 6 3 *